Robert Oster

Smoke & Mirrors

This is a work of fiction.
All of the characters names, incidents,
organizations and dialogue in this novel
are either the products of the author's
imagination or are used fictitiously.

TABLE OF CONTENTS

Bobcatbooks
@bobcatbooks.Net

Chapter One

<u>Pick of the Litter-box</u>

Hire the laziest candidate from those with the highest talent.
Lazy employees usually find a way to get the work done quickly.
Corman B. Van Dyke, <u>Successful Hiring Practices</u> (1951)

Monday, April 4, 1955, 10:45 AM
NUC Conference Room - Second Floor
National Underwriters Consortium Building
1151 Connecticut Ave. NW, Washington, DC

All twenty new employees left the group orientation meeting to go to their assigned offices located on the third and fourth floors. NUC was conducting an experimental project by which each member company would lend out one insurance investigator to work on unsolved nationwide insurance investigations in teams of two. Twenty employees from twenty companies would be rotated into the N.U.C. Special Fraud Investigation Task Force every three years.

Ben Howard wondered which one of the other nine insurance investigators leaving the elevator on the fourth floor was his designated teammate. No one followed him to his assigned office. *Perhaps my new teammate made a wrong turn*, he thought.

Ben sat alone in Room 417 for over ten minutes waiting for his new partner to join him. The 7 x 10 windowless office was cramped with two facing desks and a large file cabinet. A telephone, typewriter and lamp, along with customary office supplies and materials were on top of green desk blotters that had, **Nihil Est Per Accidens,** the NUC motto, gold stamped along its top edge. The small stack of file folders spanning the gap between the two desks reminded Ben of a travel movie he saw in which peasants were transversing two mountains across a dangerously swaying narrow bamboo bridge high above swirling craggy rapids.

Ben checked the wall clock. It was close to fifteen minutes since he entered his new work environment. But still no partner. Rather than feeling antsy that his teammate had still not arrived, boredom lulled Benjamin Howard into his usual late morning daydream reverie.

I wonder if my boss, Mr. Peters, was just trying to get rid of me when he chose me as the loaned-out employee or because he really believed I was the right person for this job. Must be the former. I was never the top performer at Quibble Surety Company. He may have thought this was an acceptable way to push out the nephew of the company's President.
Perhaps it was Uncle Ralph himself who approved of or even suggested the three year term of exile from QSC's New York headquarters after I botched the five million dollar Kow-Lique Ice Cream Company arson investigation.

Whatever the reason for the glad-handed forced expulsion, the cold hand slap of reality jolted Ben in the realization that he was living 230 miles from the glamour and glitter of New York City.
Maybe here in the nation's capital I have a second chance to make a first impression by doing the best work possible.

"How long ya goin' to sit there with your eyes closed and your kisser between your mitts?" a brash feminine voice called out.

Chapter Two

<u>How Dee Do?</u>

*Vernon and Bernice were madly in love. They might
have had a future together If it wasn't for personality
differences; He had no personality and she had too much.*
Xavier De Cordoba, <u>A Toxic Affair</u>, Kelvin Film Studios, 1937

Ben turned his head to address the sharp tongued woman. Surprisingly, she was not what he expected; lovelier than the coarse snide sound her voice suggested. Attempts to speak up came out as halting stammers. He slammed his knee into the bottom of his desk as he stood up from his chair.

While he was yelping in pain, the woman stared at him as if he were an injured cockroach writhing on its back. Then she matter-of-factly explained, "Sorry to have startled you. We'll be working together. Got here late because Mr. Fenton made an error...put three of us together in room 429. Guess I lost the bet and was sent here. Kinda think that's a good thing though. Now we have a mistake we can lord over old man Fenton should either of us screw something up."

"Oh..er-um...I, I'm...that is, my name's Ben...Benjamin Howard...from **Quibble Surety**, uhm...New York. And you are...?"

"Selma Sachs, **Inkblatt Indemnity**, Newark, New Jersey. Nice to meet you."

"Uh, if you don't mind me saying so, Selma, You don't sound... that is, you have a very pleasant voice but when you..."

"You mean my impersonation of Vivian Francis as Bowery Betty in last year's <u>Deadly Dame</u>? Love those crime and detective films!"

"Oh, me too! Must have something to do with the kind of work we do in real life."

"Don't know about you Benny, but this isn't the life I was hoping for. I've been trying to get a part in a Broadway show since I was a teenager. Only that my stepfather, Curtis Inkblatt, insisted I go to secretarial school. Then, when I graduated, he made me work in his company's typing pool. But I fooled him real good. Using my share of the life insurance money my real dad left, I took college night classes at **Zazu Pitts University** and graduated with a business degree with a minor in theater arts. That's why he sent me here. I never went out on any investigations. Guess you're stuck with me old boy!"

"Can't truthfully tell you you'll learn anything from me. I'm not very good at this game...or anything else I ever tried my hand at."

"If you don't mind me being frank, Benji, I can see why. You're all runaway nerves and...and no matter how well dressed you are, you still look like a skittish sad sack. See? Look down. Your fly is open. Must pay attention to the smallest details...like your shirttail hanging outside your pants. Very sweet looking...um, kinda like a lost lamb. Problem being, people in the business world are wolves who love to devour lamb chops like you."

"So now what....what do we do? We're two misfits in a national trade organization that expects excellence and efficiency."

Selma picked up the five file folders and replied, "Hmm. We have some cases to tackle. Let's get started and let the chips fall where they may. Here. Pull one out and we'll dive in. You know, Benji-baby, we may have a couple of advantages over those other experienced investigators."

"Like what? A nagging feeling of doom and gloom don't seem to me to be advantageous in any of life's venues. Just sayin'."

"Not knowing anything puts us on a different track. For years, those guys have been working inside a formulaic box. We have no box, no inhibitions or rules of combat to keep us from finding facts with...with a completely different perspective. Okay, what's in that folder you chose?"

"Nutty Nathan's Wholesale Grommet Warehouse. Looks like millions of dollars have been paid out over the years in slip and fall cases in dozens of Nutty Nathan's sites. Past investigations found no safety hazards or governmental safety infractions. Clean bill of health for his discount warehouses but not so for the numerous broken legs, amputated arms, fractured clavicles and even...even deaths."

"Oh, that's the guy who screams on late night TV commercials about selling a large variety of grommets at the lowest possible prices!" Selma squawked. *"Nutty Nathan The Grommet King!"*

"Yup!" Ben agreed. "He yells like a madman, ***Prices so low I'm practically giving them away! Grommets in all types and sizes! Rubber, plastic, steel, copper, nickel, zinc! We carry any variety to meet your grommet needs! Come down to one of our wholesale warehouses and see for yourself!***"

Chapter Three

<u>Crazy Like a Fox</u>
*I sell gasoline. I make a small profit. With that
I buy groceries. The grocer makes a profit. We
call it earning a living. You may have heard of that.*
Robert Mitchum as Jeff Bailey, <u>Out of the Past</u> (1947)

Monday, April 4, 1955, 11:45 PM
Apartment 2B - Living Room
3238 Wisconsin Ave. NW, Washington DC

Ben went straight to his bedroom after turning off the living room TV. He dialed Selma from his nightstand telephone.

"Is is that you Ben?" she asked, talking over Ben's *hello.*

"Did you catch the Nutty Nathan commercial?"

"Sure did. Don't know why you insisted we…"

"Yeah, I know. But the reason I…In those commercials he's always flailing his hands and arms around rapidly like…like a lunatic. So I tried focusing on the real fast one…his left hand."

"Okay Sherlock, what did you see?" Selma asked. "Was he palming some steel grommets? I didn't catch a thing."

"That wild man has four fingers on his left hand! Must be some interesting story that goes with that. I know what you're going to say, that…that he didn't have…never filed an industrial accident claim himself. But it very well could have something to do with all of the others. So many employees losing fingers…it just doesn't smell right."

"What *does smell right* to me, *Sam Spade*, is a good night's sleep. Hope to see you at nine A.M. tomorrow....fresh as a daisy wearing an unstained tie, your shoes shined with the laces tied and your fly zippered up. Goodnight Nancy Drew."

"Goodnight, Selma."

*

Monday, April 4, 1955, 11:53 PM
Anacostia Commercial Laundry Services
2201 Railroad Avenue SE, Washington, DC

Brewster Piffle was anything but a meek diminutive figure of a man. Why he chose that alias no one ever dared inquire. How Thurston Lambro was able to cross the the U.S. border under his newly assumed identity in 1948 remains a mystery as well.

The only thing soft about Brew Piffle was his voice. His hush toned speech served only to give him a more menacing presence for which any other party would not have the temerity to dispute. Yet, in all of his dealings he maintained a reputation of being fair and efficient. *Fair and efficient* didn't mean he was necessarily kind to anyone who crossed him, attempted to pull a fast one on him, on any of his close business associates or loyal employees. He expected and exacted a fair exchange for

13

all personal wrongdoings and insisted on reparations for inter
ference in his financial interests.

The latter was just the reason he was paying an unannounce
visit to local mobster Tardo Lutz. Lutz's office was located on
the top floor of a large red brick factory building within which
more than just cleaning dirty restaurant and hotel uniforms
kept Lutz in luxury's lap.

Piffle was accompanied by one of his best men whose prior
career name had been Duke "Potato Masher" Griffen, a form
boxer and part-time bodyguard. *The Mash* worked his way up
the organization by carrying out the most difficult and risky as
signments without quibble or complaint. It also didn't hurt
that Griffen had been a younger neighborhood kid that the
former juvenile delinquent, Thurston Lambro, took under his
wing when they were growing up in Toronto's seedy Moss Par
section of town.

The Mash parked his boss's black Buick Roadmaster parallel to the building's employee entrance along a dark side street. The two men waited several minutes when the laundry workers would be leaving and the throng of workers on the midnight to six shift would be pouring inside; a perfect camouflage for the Potato Masher to enter the building and creep silently up the emergency staircase to the third floor. Through the landing door's small wire reinforced window The Mash could see a tough looking gunman leaning against the wall adjacent to Lutz's office door. Duke waited for the ideal moment to make his move. The bodyguard turned his back to the stairway door and bent over to light a cigarette. It all happened in a matter of seconds. The unsuspecting goon had no time to react to Duke Griffen's brass knuckled fist which rendered him unconscious.

Duke removed the fallen man's holstered gun and a gravity knife from his jacket. Using his powerful frame, he slammed open Lutz's office door startling Lutz who had been in some sort of discussion with his numbers-man, Vig Fornulli. The mobster's bookkeeper fell to the floor holding up his trembling outstretched hands protectively in front of his face. Tardo Lutz was too tardy making a move to grab a pistol from the desk draw. The gravity knife that landed on top of the desk vibrated like a chorus of hummingbirds. Realizing that there was now a gun pointed directly at him Tardo attempted to laugh it off by saying, "Hey, Duke, heh-heh...did I say something to get you so angry at me? You need dough? Is that it? I'll get you some dough but...but you'll have to wait for Vig here to get to the safe in the room next door. Isn't that right Vig? We're all friends here Duke. You know you didn't have make such a grand entrance...coulda called in advance...woulda met you in a restaurant instead of at this..."

"You finished talkin' yet?" Duke growled.

"Well, I was about to propose an arrangement where you and I might come to some terms regarding…"

BAM! Duke slapped Lutz across his face with the force of two-by-four

"You're gonna be quiet…like your man lying on the floor outside. Only difference is he can't hear nothin'…won't even hear nothin' but ringing in his ears if and when he does come to… maybe in an hour or so. You and your bookkeeper here are going downstairs with me…for a little ride and..and some nice conversation with my boss. Seems you got some explaining to do for putting your beak a little too deep in the water."

Duke Griffen picked Vig up by his jacket and carried him like a gym bag while escorting Tardo Lutz down the metal emergency stairs and outside into the street. Duke shoved Tardo into the Buick's back seat. Brewster Piffle blew a thick cigar smoke cloud in Tardo's sweaty face and quietly snickered as if he had just landed a large sea bass after hours of fishing.

Duke *Potato Masher* Griffen deposited Vig Fornulli into the Buick's spacious trunk where he proceeded to gag and hogtie his smaller catch-of-the-day. Before slamming the trunk shut, Duke told Vig, "Remember what they say in their advertisements, *Buick: The new symbol for quality in America*!"

Chapter Four

<u>Hassles in the Air</u>

*Be careful who you call your friends. I'd rather
have four quarters than one hundred pennies.*
Al Capone

**Tuesday, April 5, 1955, 2:53 AM
Amalgamated Job Lot Commodities Corporation
551 Twixit Road, Lothian Woods, Maryland**

Duke Griffen drove his boss and their prey across the Maryland state border some 25 miles east along Route 4. He made certain he did not exceed the speed limit. Mr. Piffle always instructed his employees:

Being pulled over by local police for speeding or any minor traffic infraction would certainly be most injudicious. There's no-one more curious than a rozzer, 'specially in the late morning hours. And remember, there are always some straight coppers that wouldn't accept a bribe for looking the other way.

Naturally, in order to conduct a seemingly 100% legitimate enterprise, Piffle had numerous well placed law enforcement and judicial personnel on his payroll throughout his bailiwick, the greater capital region. *That's the price of doing business,* was his usual rationale for budgeting thousands of payoff dollars which would find their way into the pockets of poorly paid civil servants.

The AJLC building was a sprawling two story structure nestled from view within a densely wooded area. Tardo Lutz and Vig Fornulli were marched down the enormous building's outside delivery ramp leading to the basement level. They were ushered into an empty cement block room. *Shoved inside* would be a more accurate description.

Staring daggers, Brewster Piffle grabbed Tardo by his lapels and said, "I'll deal with you in a bit. But first a little demonstration of how our organization deals with sneaks who plunder our coffers...just for your education and my amusement."

"Bu...b, b, b...but Boss, I...I had no idea he was... That's what I was talkin' to him about when your Mr. Griffen busted down my office door. I was ready to put a bullet in Vig's head until he barged in."

"Maybe you did, and more likely, maybe you didn't have your fingers in the cookie jar. But that little twerp cooked the books on your watch...so's you gotta pay. I haven't decided how or what." Addressing The Mash, Brewster continued, "Okay Mash. Work Mr. Funny Money over. Go kinda light on him. We need him to look presentable when he reports for work at World-Wide Grommet Fabricators on Thursday as Andrew Throckmorton, the new stamping machine operator. I predict that he'll have a very nasty machine operating mishap."

"Sure Boss. I'll try not to break any bones...just bruising where it can't be seen...like this!" The Mash announced as he went work on Vig Fornulli.

*

Tuesday, April 5, 1955, 1:18 PM
Nutty Nathan's Wholesale Grommet Warehouse
7605 Macarthur Boulevard, Cabin John, Maryland
"Is this right? Am I correct you told my clerk that you're from our insurance carrier?" the perplexed Customer Service Manager, Edwin Stiffler asked the even more perplexed man and woman. "But your card says...both your cards say you're both Special Investigators from NUC, an insurance industry lobby organization."

"Correct, Mr. Stiffler," Selma replied while reading Stiffler's name tag. "Why did your sales clerk send us to speak to you? We're not here to return merchandise. We came here because this is the flagship location…The first Nutty Nathan's Warehouse. The corporate name's on…It's in the phone book at this very address."

"But the company headquarters are in Delaware," Stiffler replied. "You should know that if you're seasoned investigators. I can't help you. You should call NCEC, The National Cringle & Eyelet Corporation. Afraid I don't have the address. We get paid bi-weekly by check directly from from The Glen Echo Bank & Trust. Same goes for the other three warehouse stores in suburban D.C; two in Virginia and one other in Lothian Woods, here in Maryland."

"Well, um…We came here to find out…to meet with…" Ben was stammering, perhaps because he never could spontaneously respond with followup questions to statements he didn't anticipate. So Selma jumped in for the save.

"Mr. Stifler, we anticipated speaking to the owner of Nutty Nathan's…Mr. Nathan himself. Assumed he had an office at this location," Selma smiled.

Edwin Stiffler chuckled, "Hey! You guys can't be from around here, that's for sure. Otherwise you'd know that there's no real person named Nutty Nathan!"

"You think we're nuts, Mr. Stiffler?" Benjamin Howard angrily interjected. "Of course we didn't think his first name would be *Nutty!*"

"No, no sir...no miss. I wasn't making fun of you. The man in the commercials is an actor. Actually he's a well known local comedian. He's the weekend Emcee downtown at *The Obelus Club*, 5 'F' Street. Does a comedy routine as well as present different..."

"Oh, I see," said Selma. Thank you for your time Mr. Sniffler. Come on Benji. Let's get going."

"Oh, wait a minute. Here's a complimentary gift box of our # 357 eyelets...for your troubles. And the name's Stiffler."

"Yes, of course. Thank you so much. I'm sure these will come in handy some day," Selma responded.

"Goodbye, hope you enjoy them," Edwin shouted at the departing Investigators. "That's our most popular line and size!"

Stiffler waited a few minutes to make certain the two visitors had driven off before rushing to a phone in the backroom. He dialed the part-time inventory clerk's desk phone. "Hello, It's me Eddie. Two people were here sniffing around. Yes, that's right. Let me give you the details."

Chapter Five

<u>Battle of the Bulge</u>

I am not fit for this office and never should have been here.
Warren G. Harding

Selma told her partner while they were walking to the car, "I'll take the wheel this time, snookums. The way you handle a vehicle, I'm not so sure we won't be victims of some accident ourselves."

She held her hand out while Ben fumbled for the keys. "It's in your pants pocket, for heavens sake! The other pocket! Here let me get…"

Ben twitched nervously when Selma slid her hand into his left side trouser pocket to pull the car keys out. "Oh, my!" he squeaked.

"Whatsa matter?" Selma asked "You don't like being touched by a woman? Say, this is all business between us. I wasn't making a move on you, buddy, if that's what you're fantasizing."

"Er-um-uh, it…it's…just that I never…I don't know many women…not been on a…not even…never even had a woman friend."

"Well, judging from that bulge in your trousers, it can't be that you're…that you're *not* attracted to women. What work did you do before your uncle gave you a job? A monk? A priest? Should I address you as Brother Benjamin? Father Howard?"

"No, I was a specialist…ten years as the frozen pea tester at Inuit Frozen Foods…in Yonkers, New York."

"A what?"

"I mainly had the responsibility of checking the temperature of the peas before they were packed…boxed up for transport to various supermarkets throughout the country. Very lonely job…and boring. I had to wear protective clothing so I wouldn't contaminate the produce. They hired me out of high school because I worked there part time on weekends and full-time during the summers…to help support my elderly widowed mother. Had no time for friends or a social life."

"Oh, you poor dear. I'll need to find someone I know who can teach you to be a bit more…uhm, *manly*. I refuse to stand by and let you go on in life a frightened schlemiel while we're working partners. Problem is that I don't know anybody in this town. Must be some equally awkward gal in the NUC Building with whom I can put you together…introduce you. Meanwhile, I'll be getting in the car and checking through the maps in the glove compartment. We can set out on a long road trip just as soon as you feel you're physically able to sit down on the front seat next to me in a gentlemanly fashion…to put it politely."

Ben opened the passenger door and sat down. Selma started the engine. It took a few tries. "NUC must assign the oldest company cars to the temps," she pointed out.

"You said a long road trip. The office's only twenty five minutes from here. And if we go to visit the comedian who plays Nutty Nathan on TV…the nightclub won't be open and he's there on the weekends."

"Of course not, Dr. Watson," Selma smirked. We're off to beautiful downtown Martinsburg, West Virginia."

"West Virginia?" Ben yelped. "Why? Must be at least a ninety minute or two hour drive from here."

"Why, you ask? To visit *The Dibble Indemnity Company* at 1825 Queen Street, of course. You did notice that all five of our cases were insured by DIC, didn't you? "

"Er, to be honest, no. Had to memorize *The New York Department of Agriculture Frozen Food Inspection Manual* every morning for ten years. Reread it before I left for work. I hate reading reports."

"Well, we need to look through DIC's official records...at least the files on Nutty Nathan's Warehouse insurance claims."

"Uh, do you think we could stop for lunch soon? I didn't have much for breakfast," Ben sheepishly asked. "Besides, I got kind of a weak bladder."

"Sure. Hungry myself. But no coffee for you buddy. I'd like to get there directly before they roll up the Martinsburg streets."

Chapter Six

Empty Sleeve

Death is the solution to all problems. No man - no problem.
Joseph Stalin

Tuesday, April 5, 1955, 1:33 PM
Farfel B. Fenton's Office
National Underwriters Consortium Building
Unsettled Member Claims Department
1151 Connecticut Ave. NW, Washington, DC

Mr. Fenton's Private Secretary, Corvina Wuff, opened her boss's door. "Call for you, sir," she announced. "Says he's Harmon O'Leary from D.I.C. What should I tell him? That you're not in?"

"No. Please patch him in. And hold all calls for the rest of the afternoon *Corvie*. This may require a lot of discussion. Just a second. My wife will be playing bridge at the country club tonight. I'll be over at seven-thirty. Wear that thing I bought you."

Farfel Fenton, Vice President of NUC's U.M.C. Department pressed button number three on his telephone. As soon as the party on the other end picked up he whispered loudly into the mouthpiece, "Why were you calling here? We usually meet at some designated spot to exchange information and..."

"Emergency, Lefty." The voice answered. "A minor one at that if...if'n we can track down the two stooges you put on the D.I.C. cases."

"They're incompetent boobs. What harm could they do? I carefully vetted all of the candidates and chose the worst of the worst to work on those cases. And don't call me Lefty!"

"Get it into your head! Benjamin Howard and that Sachs broad just might get lucky. Those two desperate screw-ups might be desperate enough to actually do some real investigation work and if...and if anything negative comes of it...Mr. Piffle might have your right arm hanging on his living room wall just to complete the set. Got it? Now find those two schlubs and reassign them to some busywork for the time being. We'll get a couple of our inside guys to come in and write the reports negating any need for new inquiries into the any of DIC's prior claims payments."

"Sure. Have them come directly to my office and...and make sure they look the part this time. A couple of years ago the security guard threw your men out of the lobby. They looked like they were costumed for a revival of <u>Guys and Dolls</u>. Only, I have no idea where those two pathetic nitwits are. Just know they took their company car to do some work in the field. My bet is that they're probably at a matinee munching popcorn in a nice air-conditioned movie theater."

"We have some general idea what they've been up to and it smells bad," Harmon reported. "Eddie at the Nutty Nathan Warehouse called us just in time for me to send out one of our *fixers*. He said he saw them driving from the parking lot north on Thomlinson Avenue...most likely heading for Seven Locks Road. Our fixer's going to wait a bit further north in The 7 Locks Diner's parking lot and...and tail them from there when he spots the 1939 mustard brown Studebaker."

*

1:28 PM
The 7 Locks Diner
6703 Seven Locks Road, Cabin John, Maryland

Kiel Shigella waited facing the street from a parking space alongside the diner's entrance. The formerly repossessed mustard colored Studebaker was easy to spot as it backfired its way into the mostly empty parking lot. *The two subjects* got out and walked into the diner.

"Those two jokers will probably be in there for awhile eating lunch. So I got at least thirty minutes," Kiel thought.

Making certain no one was around, he opened the Studebaker's hood and disconnected the starter's power cable. He returned to his car to wait for Benjamin Howard and Selma Sach to leave the restaurant and attempt to fire up the engine.

Ben thought that Selma was uncharacteristically quiet while they were waiting for their lunch orders to arrive.

I wonder what she's thinking about, Ben thought. *Probably trying to find some nice way to get reassigned with somebody more her style.*

All of a sudden Selma asked Ben, "The other day we all saw

Mr. Fenton up on the stage introduce the orientation speakers. Anything odd about him catch your eye, Benji?"

"Well, now that you mention it...and it was only...he appeared for a few minutes and left, but...but he never faced...at least his body wasn't turned towards the audience. We only saw his face...His head...He was standing sideways. Only his right side was visible."

"Right as rain, old chum. But I got an opportunity to see him up and close when he walked me to our office after discovering I was mistakenly put together with two other Investigators. It must be an embarrassment for him but I don't understand why it would be such a big deal."

"What was an embarrassment, Selma? You saw a mustard stain on his left sleeve?"

"No you ding-a-ling! Fenton has only one arm. His empty left suit sleeve was tucked in his side pocket. He caught me staring for a second, so he explained that he lost his arm in the war. Then I was just thinking, *what war could that have been?* He had to have been a kid during World War One and...and too old to serve in the Second World War. Very curious, don't you think?"

"I think you think too much. The man's a high powered executive and we're his underlings. Let's just be concerned with getting ourselves some Brownie points for cracking the Nutty Nathan case. Okay?"

"Bravo for you Mr. Howard. You're finally speaking your piece and expressing an opinion of your own, even though I think you're not grasping the point I was making. But, okay. Let's just get this task over with...*with dispatch*, as Sherlock Holmes would say. Oh, here comes our food!"

2:35 PM

Selma tried starting the Studebaker several times. The first time she heard high pitched screeching coming from under the hood. Before attempting to start the car for a third time she instructed Ben to "...*open the hood and take-a-look-see.*" The noise was now more of a mishmash of whirring and clicking .

Ben stuck his head through the open passenger window. "What do you expect *me* to do Sel?" he asked. "I can't even make a three minute egg without some kitchen disaster taking place. We gotta get this hunk of junk towed."

"But towed to where? It's not our car. Wait! There must be emergency or breakdown instructions in the glove compartment. It's a damn company car after all."

Ben opened the passenger door and fumbled through all the papers in the glove compartment. "Here they are! I'll go in the diner and call the closest tow company on the list from one of the pay phones."

"But how will we get back to the office? I haven't seen any taxicabs around here."

"We'll think of something. Maybe someone from the office could pick us up."

"Good afternoon Miss," Kiel Shigella said tipping his hat. "I was just about to leave in that car over there when I heard your car's engine noise. I used to own five Chevy dealerships... so I know a little about auto mechanics...heh-heh, just enough to be misinformed, you might say. But from the sounds coming from your engine compartment and the fact that this looks like a poorly maintained fifteen to twenty year old junker, my guess is that your starter motor is shot. New one would cost more'n the car is worth."

"Thanks. But that's not our worry, Mister...Mister?" Selma cooed. "It's a company car and my coworker just went to call the towing service. Now we need to get a cab back to town."

"I was just about to drive into town myself. Sure would be glad to give you fine people a lift. Anywhere you need to be. Would hate to leave you in the lurch since I'm headin' in the same direction. Name's Hayden. Dorsey Hayden, Miss...Miss..."

"So very nice of you Mr. Hayden. I'm Selma...Selma Sachs."

Benjamin returned from the diner. "Tow truck will be here in three minutes," he reported. "Bad news is that we have to catch the bus three blocks away and then transfer to two others."

"Never mind about the bus Benji! This is Mr. Hayden. He offered to drive us to the office."

Ben couldn't help notice the way Selma was eying *the angel of the road*, Mr. Hayden. He shook the stranger's powerful hand and stammered, "Ni...nice to may...to make your acquaintance, sir, And, uh, thank you so much."

Selma flashed a kittenish grin and added, "We've had a very difficult afternoon Mr. Hayden. Really appreciate your assistance. Hope I can...we can repay you someday. "

"Glad to be of service. Helping others in need is its own reward, don't you agree?" The Fixer responded. "I like fixing other people's problems. This is a rather easy one."

Chapter Seven

<u>Death is in the Driver's Seat</u>
Earth's a howling wilderness,
Truculent with fraud and force
Ralph Waldo Emerson

3:10 PM

Except for his annoying adenoidal snoring, Selma felt fortunate that Ben had immediately dozed off in the backseat. This gave her the opportunity to surreptitiously inch her way across the front bench seat closer to Dorsey Hayden. Selma had been *disarmed* by Mr. Hayden's courtly deportment, his powerful build and unconventional ruggedly handsome looks. It also didn't hurt that he was well heeled. Selma made it a point to check that Dorsey wasn't wearing a wedding ring when he opened the front passenger door for her. *Mmm. That Dorsey is fair game*, she thought.

Dorsey turned for a quick look at the cute blonde woman next to him. Returning her smile he asked, "You from around here Miss Sachs?"

"No, New Jersey...which might as well be another country, far as I'm concerned. I like it here."

"Me neither. Born and bred in Chicago. Moved here a short while back to manage my grandaddy's buildings after he got real sick. That happened to be right after my partner bought out my half of our last two Chevy dealerships. Gramps passed away and I inherited all of his properties. That's how I spend my days...collecting rents and supervising my property management team."

"I see. If you don't mind my asking, how do you spend your nights? Are you married? Spoken for? Must have women chasing you from here to Timbuktu."

"Not for sometime. Haven't met a woman that I find attractive enough to want to settle down with. You see, I've already sown my wild oats...years ago, and feel the need for constant companionship with a loving and caring woman. What good is all my money if I can't share it with someone I love?"

"I'm sure that woman will appear when you least expect it. You're quite good looking, so very thoughtful and...so I would imagine you're bound to discover the girl of your dreams."

"Maybe I already have Miss Sachs. I hope you won't be offended by my brash...I mean, I'm not some kind of wolf on the hunt and...and you seem so gentle and understanding and wholesome and...and I'd like to take you out and show you the nightlife here in the DC area."

"That would be most...Yes, I would like to get to know you better myself. Give me a second and I'll write my phone number on the back of my business card. There. I'll stick it in your jacket pocket."

Selma was a little startled by what she felt as she put the card in his suit jacket. "Are you carrying...is that a gun...a, a pistol inside your suit jacket?"

"Of course it is. What with all the cash I often carry around, I need protection of some kind."

"Sorry, of course. You know, where I grew up, the only folks I knew who carried firearms were cops and...and mobsters."

"Not me. I'm too much of a coward to be a law enforcement officer and I've never run afoul of the law."

"Say, Dorsey. I need to ask. I know I don't know my way around these parts but judging from the position of the sun… Why are you driving in a northerly direction…away from the city?"

"Well, kinda a shortcut. We're taking this fractious route for two reasons. Number one is that we'll hook up onto River Road North for a short spell and then turn south onto Bradley Boulevard heading straight through the heart of D.C. This way we'll avoid the late afternoon traffic. Secondly, we'll be passing one of my buildings. A commercial property about an eighth of a mile ahead. I need to have a short word with the maintenance crew about complaints from two of the tenants. Shouldn't take more'n three or four minutes. You folks are welcome to come with me…stretch your legs. I'd like that very much Selma. Very much indeed."

"How can I refuse? Besides, I'm more than certain that Benjamin will need to use the bathroom facilities after all that ice tea he consumed."

*

3:20 PM
831 Rising Ridge Road, Potomac, MD

Ben woke up just as Dorsey Hayden (Kiel Shigella) parked his Cadillac in front of a small three story office building. "What? Where are we?" he squalled.

Selma turned around to calm her high strung coworker. "It's okay, Benny-boy. We're going into Mr. Hayden's building so he can speak to one of his employees and you can relieve yourself. Hopefully you haven't already done that Buttercup."

"No, no. I'm fine. Musta fallen asleep. What time is….oh, it's just…we only left a short while ago…the diner. Unless my watch is running slow."

"No sir, Mr. Howard," Dorsey said assuringly. "See the clock on the dashboard? We'll only be a few minutes. Then, I'll have you folks back in your office before you can say Jack Robinson. See that man waiting in front of the building? That's my chief maintenance engineer. Ha! Give a fancy title to a janitor makes him feel important. Come on folks, let me introduce you to Mr. Gauntly. Been working for Hayden Property Management Company going on forty five years…same age as this here building…Grandpa Prescott's first real estate investment."

"Hi-ya Frank. Brought along a couple of friends with me. Maybe they can help us sort this problem out," Hayden told the old man.

"What problem is that Dorsey?" Selma asked. "I don't do windows," she chuckled.

"No ma'm," Frank Gauntly replied. "Nuttin' like that. The three tenants, the insurance agency on the first floor, the trav-el agent on the second and the accountant on the third floor have all been complaining that whatever we've been using to clean and polish the furniture is leaving a sickening sweet chemical smell. What with my allergies, I can't detect a thing. Follow me down the stairs to the basement supply room."

Once inside the supply room, Frank brought out an unmarked spray bottle and two fresh cleaning rags. He sprayed the color-less liquid onto each rag and gave one to Mr. Hayden. "Mr. Hayden, why don't you have Miss Sachs see if she can smell anything unpleasant on your rag and I'll have Mr. Howard smell this one."

It took no time at all for the two NUC investigators to suc-cumb to the chloroform soaked towels placed over their faces.

Chapter Eight

Sham Fisted

*I'm here about the dead body you discovered last night,
Detective Finnegan. The body on the floor was mine.*
Kip Hastings as Lync Prentiss
<u>Swindlers Row</u>, Vertex Pictures, (1952)

3:43 PM

Frank Gauntly, known in some circles as Frank The Shiv, was transporting Selma and Ben's anesthetized bodies upstairs to the first floor on a platform hand truck. He waited at the emergency exit door for Kiel. Kiel would be injecting the two subjects with a sedative. Then they planned to place the zonked out duo under a tarp on the Cadillac's back seat.

Meanwhile, Kiel Shigella placed a call to Farfel Fenton from one of the insurance agency's telephones. As the the local Dibble Indemnity Company Sales Manager, Orson Ryebrot was always very accommodating.

"Say, Mr. Fenton, Kiel here," Shigella announced. "Yeah, yeah, took care of everything. No, job's not complete quite yet. Why? I hoodwinked those two idiots by disabling the car and offering them a ride. Made a stop at our Potomac location where The Shiv and I tricked them into breathing some chloroform. They're still sleeping like babies. Now all we gotta do is..."

"What? What were you thinking? I told you to go about this piece of business gingerly...nothing violent. I need those two here alive and well so I can keep them working on some nonsense tasks in this building...right under my eyes. What did you plan to do? Hurry! I need them here in my office before closing time!"

"Uh, well, you see...We were going to have the car...we did
have one of the guys get the car before it was towed to the
mechanic. He probably already smashed it into a tree or some
thing off the side of some remote road. I told him to toss half
empty bottles of booze inside to make it look like a drunken hi
and run diving accident."

"Oh, I guess that can be explained away by...we can get the
cops to report it was stolen by some teenagers for a joy ride
and...and crashing it. But what did you plan to do with Howard
and Sachs? Kill them and bury their bodies in one of the usual
places? That would cause all sorts of bad situations. They have
family who'd wonder what happened to them! You were very
heavy handed. Let's hope that you can fix this or you might be
one-handed. So, what were you going to do with..."

"Er, the broad fell for me. Thinks I'm a wealthy real estate
landlord. Promised her I'd take her out on the town. That's
how I got them to stop at this place...but never mind that. I
was...The Shiv and I were going to mess them up a bit like
they'd been in some drunken tussle...soak them in whiskey and
have our man at the Montgomery County Sheriff's Office,
Deputy Stockton, bring them to you. We'd have Stockton tell
you that he brought them directly to you as a courtesy, so as
not to have you embarrassed by a couple of drunken employees. Figured it would be a good reason for you to fire both of
them on the spot."

"I'll have none of that! This isn't some gangster movie. I need
them fresh, clean, stupid and naive...just the way they were
when they set foot in this building. They know too much already. You have less than two hours to clean them up and
bring them to. You'll personally take care of the girl. Keep her
occupied ....if you know what I mean. I'll figure something else
for her nervous Nellie partner. Now get going! I have to be

somewhere tonight and I don't want to be late. I want them in my office before 6 P.M. or you might be Piffled."

"Yessir. I think I know just what to do."

"Then stop talking and do it!"

Kiel sent Orson Ryebrot to fetch The Shiv and the two sleeping Nuc investigators. Selma was placed on the insurance sales office's waiting room settee and cleaned up. Ben was lying on the carpet next to her; his head resting on a chair cushion. Kiel looked at the wall clock. He estimated that it should take no longer than three to four minutes for the chloroform to wear off.

Five minutes later, Frank The Shiv was helping Ben sit up with his back against the sofa. He rushed to the water cooler and brought back Dixie Cups of cool water. Kiel was cradling Selma in his arms.

Kiel apologetically explained to Ben and Selma all about *the unfortunate accident*. Despite still being a bit groggy, they seemed to understand the jive the fake building owner was dishing out. In a matter of seconds they had re-oriented themselves to the here-and-now.

"Frank and I are so sorry for what befell you. We must also apologize to all the tenants and their employees. What was sold to us as a simple cleaning solution was inadvertently tainted."

Frank said, "Mr. Hayden, I'll contact our supplier first thing in the morning and tell them their product was emitting toxic fumes."

Kiel, laying it on thicker, added, "Even Frank and I got a little dizzy when you guys were blacking out. I'm going to have to report this all to the authorities so someone else doesn't get harmed. Might even ask my lawyers to sue _The Custer Stain & Dirt Removal Solution Company_ for all they're worth! This is outrageous!" Petting Selma's cheek he murmured, "My little darlin', you have no idea how very happy I am that you're okay."

 "Uh-oh! Quick!" Ben yelped. "Can somebody help me to the bathroom?"

Chapter Nine

<u>Hokum Powder</u>
We were together. I forget the rest.
Walt Whitman

5:52 PM
Farfel B. Fenton's Office
National Underwriters Consortium Building

"Please sit down, my friends," Farfel said to his two bedraggled and slightly bruised employees. "You've had quite a day, what with you both ending up stranded because of an unreliable vehicle and then that terrible incident with some toxic gas you told me about. But along with the bad news there is good news that came out of all of this. A turn of fortune for which I'm sure you'll both be quite pleased."

Ben tried getting the first word in but, once again, Selma beat him to the punch. "Good news Mr. Fenton? We were almost poisoned to death and...and because of what you referred to as an unreliable vehicle, we could very well have been in a terrible crash. That might have been bad enough. Yet to boot we've spent the last couple of days getting the run-around by agents for and people directly or indirectly employed by The Dibble Indemnity Company. And what have we got to show for it? I'd guess in your eyes, as a pair of insurance fraud investigators, we're a couple of losers."

"Uh, er, if I may, in our defense, um, I'd like to remind my colleague, Miss Sachs, that we did obtain a free box of # 357 eyelets. I think that very box may be the key to uncovering the whole Dibble Indemnity Company fraud scheme."

"Yes! That's it!" Fenton exclaimed. "And it's that very kind of reasoning and insight that puts the two of you high above the others. It's why I'm promoting the both of you to work as a team on more sensitive problems...internal problems here in the NUC headquarters. *Real problems* this time."

"What? What do you mean real problems this time?" Selma vociferously asked. "You mean to tell us that you sent us out on some ridiculous easter egg hunt? Why would you go to the lengths to...Why spend a load of dough to give us bogus cases to investigate?"

"Darlings, don't you see? We were testing all of our three year interns for leadership skills. I spotted the two of you right out of the starting gate. I said to myself, *Farfel, those two will be rising stars if I can guide them in the right direction*. Naturally, I assigned you five cases that have already been closed, just to see how you go about investigating a complex undertaking."

"Undertaking sounds so...so final, Mr. Fenton. We coulda died today," Ben pointed out.

"Excuse my partner for sounding so dramatic. That's what you might expect from a passionate genius of his caliber. What is it exactly we'll be doing here?"

"Well put Miss Sachs," Mr. Fenton replied. "But I have a pressing appointment to keep, so I'm afraid those details will have to wait for a few days."

"What are we supposed to do here while you're on vacation, sir?" Ben inquired.

"Ho, ho? No, my darlings. It's you two who will be going on a brief vacation. I'm giving you the rest of the week off so you can be refreshed and ready to use your energy and skills for

more important matters. Be back here next Monday. Goodnight!"

Selma and Ben watched their boss sprint out of the office.
They silently stared at each other's crumpled and rumpled
clothing, scratches and contusions.

"We look like we were run over by a steamroller!" Selma
pointed out. I gotta get out of this dress!"

While undressing Selma in his mind, Ben suggested something, the answer for which left him crestfallen. "Say, Sel. Per…
per…perhaps we oughta get back to our apartments and clean
up, er-um, get dressed to go…go out…would you mind…that is,
I really would…I'd like to go to dinner. Would like to have…for
us to…"

"Sorry buddy. I have *a prior commitment.*"

"You didn't accept an invitation from…You're not going out
with that Mister…that slick Mr. Hayden, are you? I'm sorry, you
may be…I saw how you looked at him, but…I mean, I think
he's…That Dorsey fella's not your type. There! I said it."

"My type? What do you know what my type is? An important
part of being a partner is keeping your nose out of what's not
your business!" Selma shouted. "We're workmates, not even
friends. Got it? Okay?"

Ben despondently responded, "I thought we had…we were
becoming more than…I said what I said because I'm looking
out for you the way…the way you've kind of been…how you've
been sort of protective of me. That's all. Meant no harm. I'll
leave you alone after work hours. This is just like when I was in
High School when…when all the girls went for *the bad boys*.

They called me cute but they wanted someone who looked dangerous, not adorable."

"Cuteness can be a dangerous trait in the hands of someone who's self assured. You need to find some girl who appreciates you for who you are. Sorry for you Benji-baby, that ain't me. Come, let's get out of here."

"Okay Selma Sachs. At least we can sit next to each other on the L-2 bus."

"Sure, my friend. Once I get off at Rhode Island Avenue we won't see each other until 9:00 AM, April 11th. Live with that."

Chapter Ten

<u>The Tender Trapezoid</u>

Do you ever run into that guy who used to be you?
Dave Frishberg

7:53 PM
Fusty's Coffee Shop
3301 Wisconsin Avenue NW, Washington, DC

Ben was famished but there wasn't anything to eat in his apartment. Besides, the apartment had been freshly painted the day before he moved in four days earlier on April 1st. The fresh paint smell was either making him sneeze or giving him headaches. He needed fresh air and food.

Perhaps the 1946 Kelvinator Refrigerator thought it would play an April Fool's Day joke on Ben by going on the blink around 6:00 PM the day he moved into his apartment. Ben had to throw out all the spoiled food in the refrigerator. He called the janitor the next morning who came upstairs to inspect the the dear departed long-in-the tooth icebox. The landlord's property manager called several hours later. He promised he would replace the old appliance with a new one, but there would be an additional surcharge of two dollars added to the monthly rent. Four days had passed since that sincerely worded pledge and yet the new fridge still had not been delivered.

Ben decided to have a casual meal at a fairly new coffee shop a few blocks down the street. Eating alone in a strange town was never something to look forward to. He knew he would feel more out-of-place surrounded by couples and families while dining by himself in a higher grade restaurant establishment.

Ben took a quick shower, put on some casual clothes and left

the apartment. While strolling down Wisconsin Avenue he bit
terly wondered:

*I bet that smooth-talking Dorsey Hayden will be ravishing
Selma Sachs by the time I'm sitting alone watching <u>The Red
Skelton Show</u> on TV later tonight.*

There were no customers in the small corner diner. The floor
staff outnumbered Ben six-to- one. Two cooks behind the
counter were arguing loudly about the latest Washington Sen-
ators baseball game while a busboy was busy mopping the
floor. One waitress was sitting at a back booth filing her nails
and the second waitress was showing a fashion magazine arti-
cle to the Hostess. As a local newspaper food critic said about
Fusty's:

**"The smell of stale coffee and old frying grease is so thick
at this new beanery that you could practically write on it
with a piece of chalk."**

No one paid Ben any notice except the waitress at the hostess
stand. Surprisingly, she proved to be very cordial and efficient.
The lady immediately guided Ben to a booth and signaled the
bus boy to bring water and a table setting.

Ben noticed the name *Lucy* on the waitress' name tag. Lucy
handed Ben the menu, and said, "Take your time, sir. I'll bring
you a cup of coffee. Freshly brewed."

Ben had trouble concentrating on the menu items. He was thinking about the waitress:

She seems so nice. Do I find her attractive only because she's been the first person who has spoken to me with a modicum of respect and kindness in the last week or...or is it her looks and pert personality? Sure, she isn't a raving beauty. Lucy has a nice face. And that smile! She's probably slightly older than me...certainly not a hottie like Selma. But still...

Lucy returned and placed the cup of coffee on the table. "What can I get for you, sir? It's late in the day so we're out of most specials."

Ben began to nervously stammer. He picked up the menu to point to what he wanted to eat but in doing so knocked over the entire glass of water. Half the glassful cascaded over the tabletop and onto his lap. Lucy didn't laugh, make fun or giggle as most people might have done. Instead, she swiftly withdrew a large towel from her waitress uniform sash and wiped up the wet mess. She also grabbed a handful of paper napkins from the table dispenser and offered them to Ben so he could wipe up his pants. She said, "So sorry sir. Don't be embarrassed. You aren't the first customer this has ..."

"No, Miss. I...I should apolo...apologize. You see, I...I was lost in thought...Had a terribly difficult...a very bad day today. Almost was...almost killed!"

"Oh my, sir! How awful for you. Listen, I need to whisper something to you that if Mr. Ataxia, the owner, were to hear me tell a customer he'd fire me on the spot. You seem like a nice man, so...so let me warn you...*don't order any food.* Nobody comes here...we can't get very many, if any, customers for dinner during the week. Usually college kids stop by after a ball game or movie...mostly on the weekends. We were about to close at 8:15. So the food has been sitting around for hours in warming pans…since lunch. The only thing fresh in this dive is Aldo, the short order cook. In fact, I'll be quitting at the end of the week. This place doesn't bring in enough customers to pay the rent. Fusty Ataxia's a cheap bastard…haven't seen a paycheck since the first week we opened and…and the tip money isn't enough to buy a pack of chewing gum. Speaking of chewing gum. Mildred sitting back over there, she chews and snaps gum all day. Drives me bananas!"

"Hmm. I see. Thanks for letting me know…"

"Hey, just finish your coffee…it's on the house. I made a fresh pot before you came here…just for the staff. I'll tell them that's all you wanted. Then you ought to leave and look for a more lively place that serves more…that serves edible food."

Ben looked up at Lucy with his sad puppy eyes. "Bu…but I don't know where…I jus…I just moved here…uh, from out-of-town…few days ago. I don't know any local weekday places nearby. Most of the restaurants are way downtown."

"Um, I hope you don't take this…take this the wrong way, Mister…sir…but I was planning on grabbing a bite somewhere else myself. So if you can wait around the corner for a few… maybe ten to fifteen minutes while we close this…this joint, I'll take you…show you a more suitable restaurant…nothing fancy, mind you. Besides, I hate eating alone."

"Okay, Miss…uhm…okay Lucy. I'll meet you outside…uh, around the…like you said. Very kind of you. And…and I'll skip the coffee. I really shouldn't be drinking this stuff."

Lucy flashed a sparkling smile and gave Ben a quick wink while he pressed by her and scooted out the door.

Chapter Eleven

<u>Playing with Fire</u>

Fire in the libido produces a smokey mind
Dr. A.E. Sussman, <u>Mindful Matters</u>, (1953)

Same Day - 8:55 PM
Apartment 3D
1689 N Street NW, Washington, DC

Selma had been waiting for Dorsey Hayden to arrive for over an hour. She began to feel disappointed about the man who she believed was thoughtful, caring and considerate; *The perfect future male playmate…virile but gentle.* Pacing around the apartment fully dressed for so long had her wondering if she had been stood up. After envisioning an enchanting evening on the town since she last saw him, she thought:
Men! They always disappoint, one way or the other.

Selma was about to wash off her makeup and change into her pajamas, but then the apartment building vestibule intercom buzzed like a swarm of drunken aluminum bumble bees inside a sealed tin can. Wasting no time, Selma buzzed her dream man into the building. She opened her door and waited for her date. Her heart began beating at warp speed as Dorsey Hayden exited the elevator facing her apartment. Selma was torn between wanting to hug and kiss him or excoriating him for not even calling to tell her he'd be late. Lust often tempers the natural inclinations of a person who has no problem saying directly and forcefully whatever's on their mind. And so it was when Dorsey Hayden smiled down at her and handed her a bouquet of a dozen fragrant red roses.

"Beautiful flowers for the most delicious looking woman I have ever met," he salaciously cooed.

47

Selma was convinced that the aroma of testosterone was beginning to conceal the sweet perfume of the lovely blood hued blossoms. She tried to keep calm and collected in spite of her own body's surging hormones. She stepped back as Dorsey attempted a kiss, just to keep him on a short leash. She had many techniques in her male-female kit bag to control any situation. No man ever had a chance in hell to dominate her playing field. But her life-long habit of lecturing men into submission broke through.

"You have anything to tell me, Dorsey? After all you don't keep a lady waiting. Especially on a first date. You said we'd be going for dinner and dancing at some fancy nightclub...and look at the time. I would have expected at least a phone call from my knight in shining armor. But thanks anyway for the lovely..."

BAM & FWAP! Selma fell backwards on the floor more stunned than hurt from Dorsey's open handed slaps. "Wha...?" she cried out in terror.

"No dame tells me what to do or how I should behave! You hear?" Dorsey Haden shouted. He hadn't meant to slip out of character but he couldn't abide a nagging woman bossing him around. "You little bitch. We ain't going nowhere. I got business to do tonight. Now be a good little girl. When I want to see you again, you'll hear from me!"

Selma sat up on the hard floor, shaken with tears streaming down her face, witnessing Kiel Shigella, who she knew as Dorsey Hayden, abruptly leave and slamming the door behind him. It took her several minutes to calm down enough before she stood up on her wobbly legs. The left shoulder strap of her new cocktail dress was ripped as was her heart. She ran to the bathroom and cried all the anger and fear from her system...a habit she had since her abusive childhood. She soon thought it best to get away from the apartment and perhaps get some dinner where she could thinks things out.

Sitting on the edge of the bathtub, Selma thought:
That brute tonight wasn't the man of my dreams I thought he was. He turned out to be a nightmare instead. Dr. Jekyll, no... Mr. Hyde, yes. I ought to speak to...discuss what just occurred with Benjamin. He should know and maybe be warned that we were in the hands of a crazy violent man...A man with a gun! Poor Benji. I wonder if he could ever forgive me for treating him the way I did. In a sense, I did to him what that savage lout did to me. Ben Howard is so fragile. I must make it up to him.

Selma wandered down nearby Rhode Island Avenue toward one of the several <u>Hot Stoppes</u> cafeteria style restaurants in and around the Capital region. Before entering, she spotted Ben Howard's familiar face through the plate glass window. She was thinking what words to use to greet her work partner so as not to startle and/or anger the nervous man. She thought Ben seemed so relaxed and so alone. But a woman was already sitting down at Ben's table while she was rehearsing how she might casually stop by and take the very same booth-seat herself.

Selma said to herself:

That woman must've just returned from the ladies lounge. They look like they're deep in conversation. Hadn't seen a smile on Benny's face before. Best not to interrupt...just go back and make some scrambled eggs at home, then call it a night. I'll phone him tomorrow. Maybe we can meet somewhere for lunch.

Chapter Twelve

Full Frontal Photo Op

*He dashed from one end of the Royal Palace
Ballroom to the other to see her up close; the most
beautiful woman in all of Russia. Prince Nicolai looked
deeply into Tatianna's eyes and she in his. He gently kissed
her hand. They joined the other dinner guests for the last waltz.*
Leonid Oblonsky Kuznetsov, Tsar-Crossed Lovers, (1927)

**Same Day - 8:15 PM
The Caspar Arms Apartments - Apartment 4C
2022 Columbia Road NW, Washington, DC**

Corvina Wuff was seated at the edge of her large circle bed *inflating* her boss, Farfel Fenton, as if he was a deflated beach ball. The sudden intrusion of flaring flashbulbs illuminated Fenton's mistress' dimly lit sanctorum like exploding Roman candles. Corvina turned from her task at hand and saw two tough looking men, one with a baseball bat and the other photographing the sexual activity taking place.

Corvina screamed at the top of her lungs as a third man strolled into the love nest. He was holding out a single sheet of paper.

Fenton's moaning susurrations promptly changed to a series

of terrifying gasps when he pulled off the blindfold that had been part of the evening's playtime activities. "What's going on?...Oh, no...No!"

Brewster Piffle addressed the naked NUC executive officer sotto voce, "This is the thing Fenton. You're going to take this resignation I had typed for you, sign it and submit it to the Board of Directors first thing tomorrow morning. Here, read it. It states you have an urgent family medical emergency which requires your full attention and, as such, you feel that you can no longer give your full attention to your present administrative responsibilities."

"But I tried my best to..."

"You don't stay in this game by trying your best. You stay in this game by being successful. And you don't stay at my table by squandering my operation's dough on fancy luxury digs so you can get laid behind your wife's back. Oh, and the part about an urgent family emergency ain't a lie either. As I'm speaking, your wife will be driving a certain Kiel Shigella to their favorite motel across the Potomac, The Woodland Acres Motor Lodge. They won't get far. Time bomb's set to go off any minute now. Just enough of a blast to cause a middling-size crash on the country roads of northern Virginia."

"Oh no! What have you done!" Farfel yelled. "You're a...a mon..."

"I had enough of this bum," Piffle told Sluggo Strothers, one of the goons. "Take him up on the roof and treat him to a small taste of what he deserves. I suppose losing an arm didn't make much of an impression. Ah, but that was many years ago when he was young and foolish. Hurry up Sluggo, I still got some 'portant business with this young lady. You with the camera, go downstairs and wait in the car."

Brewster smiled at Corvina as soon as the others had left the apartment. "You did good, Kitten. Keepin' an eye on that double dealer for me and going the extra mile to gain his confidence with your *feminine wiles*...I think they call it. You can keep this place. Just get rid of any trace of that Fenton character. That's an order. Here's a couple-a thousand to get new bedroom furniture...plus a little extra for being such a good kid. Tomorrow you'll be moving upstairs to the employment office as the Assistant Administrator."

"Brew, you're such a doll! Hope you have time before you go. I'm already dressed, or rather undressed, for some fun, my big teddy bear."

"Yeah, sure. Just wash up first. You got that old goat's smell all over you."

"Sure, Honey. Wanna scrub me down in the shower?"

Chapter Thirteen

<u>They Say It's Wonderful</u>

If we always helped one another, no one would need luck.
Sophocles

Same Day - 8:20 PM
Hot Stoppes Restaurant # 33
1713 Rhode Island Avenue NW, Washington, DC

Ben anticipated it would be a cordial but perfunctory dinner experience; two people who happened to meet for the first and only time breaking bread and filling no more than thirty minutes with awkward small talk. He was certain Lucy would be eager to leave as soon as they finished their plates; parting their separate ways never to set eyes on each other again. And why not? He's never been very good at improvising charming conversation or appearing to any woman he's ever tried to speak to more than a mere hapless loser. The one time he went to see a psychologist he was told, *Perhaps it's because of being reared by an overbearing and over protective elderly mother that you fall to pieces in the presence of any woman that interests you.*

But that wasn't the case this evening. Lucy's voice had a calming and reassuring affect. Within a few minutes, Ben slowly began to realize he was no longer stammering, stuttering, blabbering, babbling, blathering, fumfering or tripping over his words.

"You know Lucy, we never exchanged names. I'm Benjamin Howard."

Lucy smiled and replied, "My last name's Herzog." Holding her arm across the table for a hand shake, she continued, "Pleasure to make your acquaintance, Benjamin Howard," she smiled.

"Me too, Miss Lucy Herzog. You know, I haven't met anybody as nice as you since I've been in this town...maybe since I was born," he chuckled self-deprecatingly.

"You need to develop a little self-confidence, Benjamin. You're a nice looking man and...and I suspect you have a good heart...probably one that's been broken one too many times, which may account for the sadness in your eyes. I've had my share of heartbreak, so I know how that looks and feels. I gave up on men five years ago after a bitter divorce to a rotten abusive man."

"Sounds dreadful, Lucy."

"I'm over it now. Worst part of it all was that I gave up a good career as the President of CAARS."

"Cars? You mean automobiles?"

"No, silly. CAARS stands for *The Capital Area Animal Rescue Society*; the largest animal shelter in these parts. Growing up, I learned a great deal about business and management from working in my dad's business. And I was always bringing home injured animals to take care of. But how about you? You passed a very serious comment at Mr. Ataxia's grease pit. You said you were almost killed today. What happened?"

Ben's recounting of the day's event was more of a brief outline. He figured that he wouldn't be violating any non-disclosure agreements if he left out names, places, addresses and the purpose of his investigation.

"I see," Lucy said. "From the short sketch you just presented, I'd guess that you're some kind of investigator, inspector or examiner; That's for sure. What is it...can you tell me generally what it is you're looking for?"

Ben reached into his side pocket, pulled out and handed Lucy the small plain cardboard box. "Know what these are?" he asked.

"I should know! My dad manufactured these and other items like this for the Armed services until he was forced to close down his factory when cheap imitations began being imported to these shores. What you've handed me are # 357 eyelets. Wouldn't use these for anything. Most inferior quality...not constructed of high grade steel...definitely not carbon or even nickel steel. More like Ferronium Tishbite, the metal substituted by sleazy manufacturers during the War which caused numerous military mishaps; Cannons exploding , planes crashing and so on. Look at this. See? They have welded seams! You didn't buy these, did you?"

"No. I guess it wouldn't matter if I divulge who's employing me for the next three years. They're a big operation here in DC. You see, I was loaned out to NUC by my uncle's insurance company, Quibble Surety as a special temporary insurance fraud investigator. Began working for NUC just this last Monday."

"Okay, my turn, Ben. What's NUC? Never heard of any NUC in this town, and I've been living around here all my life."

"It's The National Underwriters Consortium. They're a lobby and trade organization for twenty of the smallest insurance companies in 20 states."

"Never heard of them. I should know them all. My ex-husband is Senator Pembroke Sneddonk ...or rather, disgraced ex-Senator Sneddonk."

"Oh, isn't he the guy who…?"

"Yeah, that's him alright! Serving 48 years in a federal prison for corruption and censured by Congress for morale turpitude. Also divorced by me for his bad attitude, philandering and cruelty. "

"Oh my! Yet you seem to have a good attitude about all that nasty business you went through, Lucy. Say, It's getting late. I'd really love…like to speak to you some more…when we can make time for a longer conversation. But you must be dog-tired..standing on your feet all day. Do you think…?"

"Yes of course. Let's get together for another chat on a day when we're both free." Lucy took her lipstick from her purse and scribbled something on one of the paper napkins. "Here's my phone number. Perhaps next Sunday we can…we can meet again. Of course, by then I'll be busy looking for a new job. Hard to get anything with my skill set in this town at my age, you know. Waitressing isn't what I'm thrilled doing."

"I wish I could see you sooner. My coworker and I were told to take the rest of the week off and report back Monday morning to begin a more challenging assignment…at the national headquarters building. I'm very curious about how you gained so much knowledge about eyelets. Not a subject area most people are familiar with."

"You were given the rest of the week off, Ben? Doesn't that seem odd to you. You just started…you started your job at NUC less than 48 hours ago and…and they're going to pay you to do nothing for three days? The dues paying members wouldn't appreciate that, would they?"

"I suppose not. But my partner and I were injured on the job. Maybe that's how they're justifying that arrangement."

"Sounds like a stretch to me," Lucy remarked. "So just to assuage your curiosity...and not to get into details right now, my father owned a thriving manufacturing company that produced precision cringles, eyelets, tiny industrial and medical tubing plus a variety of standard and custom sized grommets. I would guess that wherever you obtained that box of defective eyelets...I'd say that you must have gotten them at one of the Nutty Nathan's Discount Warehouses."

"Uh-huh. You hit the legendary nail on the proverbial head, Miss Lucy Herzog. May I walk you home?"

"No dear. It's very nice of you to offer. My apartment's only short distance from here and, since you said you live close to Fusty's, you'll need to walk in the opposite direction...then a good ways up Connecticut Avenue to wait for the L2 bus. Goodnight, Benjamin."

"Goodnight, Lucy."

Ben thought as he began walking to the bus stop, I should have asked before she left. What the hell's a cringle anyway?

Chapter Fourteen

<u>Not Up to Snuff & Snuffed Out</u>

To eat is a necessity, to dine is an art.
Betsy-Louise Perkins, Food Critic

Wednesday, April 6, 1955, 7:30 AM
Fusty's Coffee Shop
3301 Wisconsin Avenue NW, Washington, DC

Enoch Hamdinger, a DC Health Inspector for 21, years had never seen anything as dangerous as the conditions at Fusty's. He had to act swiftly to stop any of the remaining 10 breakfast customers from putting another bite of tainted food in their mouths. He rushed from the kitchen into the front of the restaurant holding up his Health Inspector badge in his right hand and the clip board DOH check-off list in his left hand shouting ***STOP EATING!***. The owner Fusty Ataxia sheepishly followed behind him.

"Ladies and gentlemen! Please put down any and all utensils and leave the premises immediately! I am officially closing down this restaurant due to finding in excess of three dozen violations of the City's cleanliness and food preparation codes. Please be sure to monitor your temperature and be aware of any abdominal cramping, pain or diarrhea. These may be symptoms of food poisoning. I would urge each and everyone of you to rush to your family physician or the closest hospital emergency room for a complete physical examination."

Inspector Hamdinger went outside and pasted a huge DOH warning sign on the plate glass window while the last several customers exited the greasy spoon. He returned inside and ordered Mr. Ataxia to put up a *closed* sign and to lock the front door. Enoch asked to meet with the entire restaurant staff during which time he singled out the kitchen staff about personal hygiene, required food preparation sanitation, daily kitchen appliance cleaning procedures and food storage and labeling rules and regulations. Then he left in a huff thinking:

I ought to buy a new set of clothes, burn the ones I'm wearing and submit a reimbursement request to my boss. Hope I can get the smell of that dead cat with a rat in its mouth I uncovered behind the stove out of my nose....and memory!

Mildred asked Lucy what she planned to do now that she was out of work. "Least I got a skill to fall back on," she smirked. Then she walked away snapping her chewing gum.

Yeah, you sure do. On your back for sure, you old whore! Lucy thought. But then she felt bad about thinking so ill of another broken human being. *Who in this world doesn't have their shortcomings? I need to talk to somebody right now!*

Lucy ran around the corner into Poisson's Drugstore to use the phone booth. She fished around for loose change and dialed the Operator. "Hello, I need the phone number for a new customer of yours...Mr. Benjamin Howard. Yes, Yes! That sounds like it would be an address nearby! Please dial his number for me, Thanks...Okay, yes....I'm putting another nickel in the.... Hello Ben! It's me, Lucy. I have a problem. Can I come to see you? Yes, *now*. Would it be okay if I...can I come to your place in a few minutes or would you rather we meet somewhere in your neighborhood? Great! I'll be right over."

Ben's Apartment

Ben hoped he had enough time to straighten up and hide all of the dirty laundry piled up on the bathroom floor. He was able to shove it all under his bed just as the downstairs inter-com began zizzing.

"Come on in Lucy," he answered. "Apartment B...second floor. Can't wait to see you!"

Chapter Fifteen

<u>Holding Pattern</u>

*Having someone wonder where you are when you
don't come home at night a very old human need*
Margaret Mead

Ben's Apartment - 8:00 AM

Ben was mildly shocked but highly gratified to have Lucy Herzog calling on him. He was taken back at first by the way she appeared at his door; not the self-confident optimistic woman he spent time with the night before. He surmised that something must have occurred at the restaurant to cause her to look so distressed because she was still dressed in her waitress uniform.

Lucy rushed into the apartment, stopped to look through tear filled eyes at Ben's concerned expression and then hugged him, pressing her head against his chest. Ben, never having the experience of a woman's embrace, was bewildered. He held his arms at his side as if he might be accused of molestation should he dare to reach around her.

"Hold me Ben. Hold me tight! I think I may fall apart into a thousand pieces if you don't. And please, lock the door. I...I might have been followed!"

Ben took that as a cue it was okay to embrace the trembling woman. "Following you? I don't understand. Something happen at work this morning that...?"

"Oh, Benjamin. I met you at the right time. I can't go to the police about all of this. I need a place to hide out for awhile. They may try to...to kill me."

  With Lucy still clinging to him, Ben walked backwards towards his small living room. He somehow managed to break her bearhug and get her to sit her down on his sofa. He handed her his handkerchief so she could wipe the tears and blow her nose. "Why Lucy, you look pale as a ghost. Calm down so you can tell me what's …"

  "Okay Benjamin, thanks. I think I'm okay now. Sort of. I had quite a scare when I was walking past the diner to get here. Fusty's place was closed down by a Department of Health inspector that Fusty probably couldn't pay off this time. I was going to quit anyway, so not working in that hell hole didn't bother me. I figured that since we both had the day off we might be able continue our discussion. I mainly wanted to help you solve *your grommet puzzle*. Last night I didn't give you the entire lowdown on Fusty's Coffee Shop."

  "Entire *lowdown*? That pla…that place was a filthy *letdown*," Ben tensely uttered to lighten Lucy's anxiety.

  "I thought when I started there it was…it seem quite unusual that Mr. Ataxia, a man who runs several other restaurants, didn't seem to be engaged…not monitoring anything that went on in his business. He'd only show up now and then to talk exclusively to Aldo, retrieve his girlfriend, Mildred Zalopé or to hand us our weekly paychecks. Well, actually he handed out envelopes of cash, which to me was a signal something crooked was going on. When I was hired, Fusty pointed out he has an arrangement with the government to take in men who have served their time in prison…*paid their debt to society*, is what he called it. Take Aldo Cattivo, for instance. Aldo learned the rudiments of cooking from working in the mess hall kitchen at The Duane Reade Penitentiary. Yet, it was Aldo who seemed to be in charge of everything from purchasing produce and meat to keeping the books…such as they were…"

"What do you mean by that, Lucy? How do you keep records on a business with a cash only payroll?" Ben asked. "Even I know something about that from sitting in on my uncle's monthly executive board meetings."

"Exactly. So one night when everything was super quiet...a rainy Friday with zero customers...which never seemed to concern Mr. Ataxia anyway...So, Aldo was sitting at the back booth going over the diner's ledger when José yelled out to him that there's a big fire...a stove fire and he didn't know where they kept the fire extinguisher. Aldo had sent Mildred home earlier so I was left alone in the front room for just enough time to flip through the books. Aldo caught me just as I was setting the ledger back on the table. He yelled something very nasty to me, which I wouldn't repeat in public, about sticking my nose where it doesn't belong. He threatened to cut my face to shreds if I ever touched the diner's record books again. I was plenty frightened but just as angry at him as he was of me. He calmed down when I explained that I was finishing wiping off the tabletops and had to pick the ledger book up to clean off the last banquette; that I didn't open it and what would I know about bookkeeping anyway. He seemed to have believed me. Then there's Mildred, who had spent time...multiple arrests and jail time for running *a house-of-ill-repute* in Baltimore. She took a great dislike to me. Don't know why. She did very little work, came in late or not at all and bragged she's *Fusty's girl*. I knew I better get out of that place. This morning's health code violation shutdown made it easier than my having to give Mr. Ataxia a personal notice of resignation. You saw for yourself last night. I would encourage customers who refused to eat the food and walked out to make their complaints to the Health Department. I was hoping that if Fusty hired a new crew we might have a going concern which would mean better tips for me. Maybe it was that creepy busboy José who overheard me saying that multiple times."

"But you said you were followed. Why do you think they want to...?"

"Mildred made some snide remark to me when we closed the joint. Later, when passing by the diner, Mr. Ataxia asked me what I was doing around the corner and...and if It was me who called Mr. Hamdinger to pay a surprise inspection. He accused me of following the health inspector to his car to give him more information about *the operation*. I said that I needed to find a place to stay because I can't pay my rent...that I went to call a friend from Poisson's Drug Store's pay phone. He was more than skeptical. He barked at me, *Why didn't you ask to use my phone right here*? That's when I ran here as quickly as..."

Ben held Lucy's face in his hands, "You're safe and sound right here, Lucy. I'll look after you. You don't have to be worried. I won't forget to feed you like I did to the dozens of goldfish I had as a kid. And this is a two bedroom apartment...or so my lease states it is. The second bedroom is more like a walk-in closet. But it's carpeted. I could sleep there on the floor and you can have my room. I hope you'll say it's okay. I don't care what nosy Mrs. Furf next door thinks."

Lucy breathed a sigh of relief. "But my things? My clothes, personal items and unmentionables are at home. I dare not go get them."

"Hmm. Maybe there's someone who I could persuade to help us in this part of our plan...my coworker, Miss Selma Sachs."

Ben dialed Selma on the kitchen wall phone. There was no answer. "Uh, she's not at home...it would seem. At least I have an extra toothbrush and you could wear one of my shirts to sleep in tonight. There'll be plenty of food once I go to buy groceries. Those thugs don't know my face. I got a call an hour ago that the new refrigerator will be delivered between 2:00 and 4:00 this afternoon."

"At least that's some good news," Lucy sighed.

Just then the phone rang. An angry male voice at the other end groused, "This is Cooper Rhanbyte! Forget Fenton. I'm your new boss. Why haven't you reported for work? You and your coworker better get your butts in my office in two hours along with a damn good explanation about one of our company cars that was found totaled on Lambeth River Road!"

Chapter Sixteen

<u>Mercy Killing</u>

Too many of us are not living our
dreams because we are living our fears
Les Brown

10:20 AM
Cooper Rhanbyte's Office
National Underwriters Consortium Building
Unsettled Member Claims Department

Cooper Rhanbyte stood behind his desk railing at the top of his lungs, "You were afforded a career changing opportunity here at NUC and...and in the first two days all you two dunderheads have done is demonstrate an utter lack of common sense and responsibility! What I have to decide now is what to do with two loose cannons who demonstrated their sheer incompetence, unreliability, carelessness and negligence by leaving a valuable NUC asset...to wit, a company automobile, at a location where it was easily stolen and destroyed by a gang of drunken teenagers!"

Selma attempted to remonstrate, "Now, just a moment, sir. That's not exactly..."

"Might I also point out, that in addition, you numskulls didn't

even show up at work today!" Rhanbyte bellowed. "I'd fire yo
both and send you packing if you weren't already employed b
two of our best member insurance companies."

As was her wont, Selma gave back as good as she got, "Sir!
What do you know about any of this except about some so-
called automobile? It was in effect a damn old worthless...a
barely running junker...a repo, for crying out loud! I'm ques-
tioning, and so should you, how a car that needed a new
starter could have actually been hot wired by some unknown
teenagers and driven to its final resting place. All said, if anyone crashed it it would have been declared a mercy killing."

"Well, that's not the poi..."

"The point is that we told you we called the closest tow company on NUC's auto insurance list. They're the ones who said i
was okay for us to leave it; that they would be there in three to
ten minutes. We were stranded. A stranger offered us a ride
back to town; We reported directly to Mr. Fenton. He told us to
take the rest of the week off. Promised us a new...a more re-
sponsible position starting Monday...right here in this building.
You must have his notes, memos, something in writing; do you
not?"

Cooper Rhanbyte sat down. Scratching his head he replied in
a softer tone, "Well, uh-um, now that you mention it. I found
nothing...nothing in writing. Fenton's former secretary, Miss
Wuff told me that she had already left for the day the time you
two may have had your little chat with her former boss. By the
way, she's under the impression that she's been promoted as
the new Assistant Personnel Manager, starting on Monday.
And there are no directives from anyone changing your or
her's employment status. Something Fenton had no authority
to do anyway."

Finding his courage, Ben finally piped up. "Excu...ar-um...excuse me Mr. Raincoat. Then where will we be working? Mr. Fenton said...he was...he explicably stated that the cases we were investigating had already been settled...that...they were given to us as a test. He heaped praise on us for what we attempted and thought that..."

Selma cut in over Ben's plodding stammering, "He said we were *rising stars*!"

"My name's *Rhanbyte*, Mr. Howard! And I don't give a rat's ass what he told you. Forget about Fenton and forget about working here...at least until we figure out what to do with the two of you. I suppose that since this isn't all...this mess Fenton left isn't entirely your doing, I will recommend to the upper ups that we put you both on *Paid Leave Status*. Don't leave the vicinity. Stay put and wait until I call you. I may be able to come up with some outside assignment you can work on for...*personally for me*...maybe as a team or separately. Just don't mention any of this to anyone. Definitely stay away from this building. I'll have Payroll mail you your paychecks. You understand?"

"Yessir!" Ben and Selma chorused, They seemingly backed out of Cooper's office as if they had had an audience with the Royal Family.

Other than shooting perplexed glances back-and-forth, Ben and Selma exchanged not one word util they were on the sidewalk in front of the NUC building.

"What now Sel?" Ben asked "What should we do? Stay beholden to that pomp...pomp...pompous blowhole...er, blowhard?"

"I say hurray! We can do whatever the hell we want as long as the paycheck's in our mailboxes every Friday!"

"Listen, okay...I know you like to have a good...good time but I have a serious problem with a woman. I need some assistance with..."

"Oh, Benji-Boy! You gotta be kidding! You think you knocked up some dame and you want me to help you find an abortion doctor? Whoever that dame is, she's playing you for the biggest sap that ever lived. No woman could know she's pregnant one day after...you know. She's trying to wrangle money out of you, my sweet naive pussycat."

"No! No! It's nothing like that. Please Selma, I need you to do a small favor. I don't want to get you involved in why this needs to be done but there are some dangerous...Um, I better not get into any details. So, would you be willing to take a short cab ride with me to this lady's apartment? See? This is her key. You won't be breaking into her place. She said that she keeps a large suitcase stowed up on the bedroom closet rack. This is a list of the things she needs. It won't take long. I'll wait in the cab while you retrieve these items, then I'll drop you off wherever you'd..."

"Although I'm quite curious about who this mystery woman is, how you came to have such an intimate relationship and what she looks like, our own mutual relationship stops at any and all intrigue, collusion with unknown persons or possible entanglement that ain't none of my personal business. So, in a word, as we say in Jersey, *Fa-get-bout-it!* You go your way and I'll go mine as planned. Right now, I intend to get my hair and nails done. Bye Benjamin! See ya in the funny papers!"

Ben was miffed. He should have known that Selma, unlike Lucy, was all about hedonistic self interest and vanity. He hailed the next passing cab, jumped in and gave the driver

Lucy's address. "I'll need you to wait downstairs for me when we get there, " he explained.

 "Hey this here ain't New York, Mister. Fares are zoned. I ain't gonna wait around. I need to get as many fares as possible."

 "What would you say if I gave you five bucks on top of the thirty five cents? "

 "Mister, you made my day! Sure."

Chapter Seventeen

<u>Little Things Mean a Lot</u>

The heart that cannot laugh cannot sing. But who knows for sure? It could be the other way around.
Leopold Switzer, <u>The Music of the Universe</u>, 1923

Ben's Apartment - 12:41 PM

While unlocking his apartment door, Ben made a mental note to give the spare set of keys to Lucy. He stood in the small foyer and looked around for signs of Lucy Herzog. For a brief moment he believed he had accidentally entered another tenant's flat. It soon became clear the apartment had been cleaned from top to bottom. The furniture had also been rearranged a bit differently.

I like what she did, he thought. *The living room looks larger without all that clutter. Doesn't smell like an old bachelor pad... as they would say on TV.*

Ben called out, "Hello. Lucy, I'm home!" There being no answer, he assumed she was taking a nap in the bedroom. Ben didn't want to disturb her after all of her hard work, and yet, he wanted to bring her suitcase into the bedroom so they could make room in his dresser for her things.

But Lucy wasn't asleep on the bed nor was she anywhere else. He began to panic.
Had they gotten to her? Is she safe?

Back in the kitchen he noticed the old refrigerator was missing.
The janitor must have been here, removed the old piece of junk to make room for the new one. Maybe he ordered her out of the apartment because...because she's not on the lease! But

wouldn't she have left a note?

Ben would soon learn that all of his borrowed worries were for naught when he heard the lock's tumbler turning, the door opening and Lucy calling, "Ben are you home yet?"

"I had quite a fright Lucy. Where were you? I just came home and...thought something terrible happened to you. Say, where'd you get that?"

Lucy dropped a large laundry basket filled to the brim with neatly folded mens clothing on the floor. She tittered and gave Ben a sweet peck on this cheek. "That's for you worrying so much about me, Benjamin. I couldn't just sit here all day being a bad guest and mooching off you. So I thought I ought to vacuum, dust and move your furniture where it would look a bit nicer. I hope you don't mind."

"No, of course not. But you didn't have to..."

"I wanted to, Silly-boy. I was getting ready to wash the dishes you left piled up in the kitchen sink when the doorbell rang. Gary the janitor was at the door to remove the old refrigerator. He said the new one will be here a bit earlier. He asked about my waitress uniform. I told him that I'm *Mr. Howard's maid.* Your next door neighbor stuck her head in the doorway to find out what all the commotion was about while Gary was pulling the old icebox into the hallway."

"You mean that busy-body, Mrs. Furf?"

"Yes. But she seems like a nice lady. Why do you dislike her?"

"She always drops by to chit chat, as if I have anything to say to her. Each time she mentions having me meet her niece, Ingrid. *You'd make such a lovely couple!* she says while shoving a photograph of Ingrid in my face.

Lucy admitted, "Well, I think she was very sweet. Just a lonely old widow. Told me the Readers Digest version of her life. But best of all, when I asked if she could lend me a laundry basket, because I couldn't locate Mr. Howard's, she ran back to her apartment and insisted I keep this one. I fished out your spare door key from the kitchen counter drawer. Then I was able to go down to the basement laundry room. I used most of he loose change I found in your sofa for the washing machine and dryer."

"You found my dirty...?"

Lucy laughed, "Benny, you didn't actually think I wouldn't discover you've been stockpiling all your...shirts, pants and underwear...been cramming your dirty clothing under the bed since...since the Bronze Age? Mrs. Furf is right. You need a woman in your life."

The door bell rang twice. Within fifteen minutes a spanking brand new Crosley Shelvador refrigerator made its home in Benjamin Howard's kitchen.

Chapter Eighteen

<u>It Takes a Tough Woman</u>

A journey of a thousand miles begins with airfare.
Thelma Buffington,
<u>Planning Your Overseas Vacation</u> (1955)

Wednesday, April 6, 1955, 11:23 AM
(earlier -the same day)
The Mayfly Hotel - Lobby
1126 Connecticut Avenue NW, Washington, DC

Selma Sachs marched down Connecticut Avenue leaving Benjamin Howard to his own devices. She felt badly having to act the role of a tough no-nonsense woman. She knew if she was to uncover the answer to a number of personal and professional questions she would have to cut loose from that sweet *farblondjet* man. She crossed the street and entered the historic Mayfly Hotel.

She thought, *What better place is there to find out about an industrial lobby than in this lobby where the movers, shakers and shake-downers all cross paths or meet for a drink or lunch with important campaign contributors and influential VIPs?*

Selma spotted a bellhop entering *The Sedgwick Bar & Grill.* She surmised from the envelope he was carrying in his white gloved hand, *Perhaps he just might be on his way to deliver an important message to someone important.*

Selma double stepped it in time to catch up behind the uniformed hotel attendant and tap him on the shoulder. Handing him two crisp dollar bills she said, "Excuse me. I'm sure you could point out at least one person in this crowded room who might know something about how the government works around here. I'm doing research for my graduate degree and I need to find out where to find out about a certain procedural.. uhm, procedure."

"Sure Miss. You're in luck today. See that silver-haired man at the bar, the good looking older gentleman drinking alone? That's Senator Winslow Tontine. Usually on the prowl...if you'll pardon my expression. The Senator usually likes to drink alone and pick up...er, find...I mean he..."

"That's alright. I get the point. And thanks for the info."

Selma knew right away from the reflection of Senator Tontine's grin in the full width wall mirror behind the bar that he likewise had caught a glimpse of her approaching his barstool.

Selma took the seat next to him, turned and smiled, "Oh my!" she exclaimed in a southern accent and with her hands on her cheeks. "Aren't you Senator Tontine from the great state of Tennessee? My Daddy voted for you five times, sir!"

"Well, aren't you a pretty young thing?" he drawled. "A flower of the South, if there ever was one, miss."

"Why thank you kindly, sir. I would seem that fate must have steered me to my home state Senator just when I'm in great need of some general procedural information for my graduate course in American Political Institutions. It's really a simple matter, Senator. I hate taking up your valuable time with such a piddling request. You see, I'm working on an advanced degree in political science right here in Washington at...at Pat Bertram University."

"Why that's a fine institution...a fine school indeed. I might also add, you must be as smart as you are lovely. What's your name little lady and what do you need to know? I'll put my entire staff at your disposal if there's something I can't answer to your satisfaction."

"My name's Lucinda Butterworth but most people just call me Lulu, Senator Tontine. I need to speak with...would like to interview the person in charge of reviewing and authorizing official lobby organization applications. Can you arrange to..."

"Most certainly. Yes, it is a very simple request which I will be a most happy to help you with. As soon as I get back to my office I will personally call The Senior Congressional Clerk, Samson Sprugg."

"Oh how gracious of you, sir. I hope I can repay your kindness someday soon," Selma cooed.

"Perhaps we can discuss your studies over some cocktails and dinner, my dear."

"I'd like that very much, but maybe sometime next month. I need to study for finals. I won't be back on campus for some time today. Can I call you directly to find out when I might pay Mr. Sprugg a call?"

"But of course, of course. Call me at 2:15. I'll be certain to tell Sammy that you won't require more than ten minutes of his time. He owes me a few favors, so I'd say you might very well be able to chat with him between three and four. Oh, I do hope you'll drop by my office when you're finished with Sprugg."

"I certainly will sir. I've never been in a Senator's private office."

"Despite the great honor and responsibility, being a Senator is a very lonely job when we're not in session during the long late afternoon hours."

"Then I'll make it a point not to forget to keep you company, sir."

"Please call me Winnie, Lulu. This may be the start of a beautiful friendship."

"Being a single small town gal in a strange city, I'd like that very much, Winnie."

3:51 PM

Selma rushed out of the Capitol Building and down the marble steps. She had gotten the information from the Senate Clerk; Information that supported her theory. The National Underwriters Consortium never was an approved lobby organization, never even applied for such a status nor had any NUC agents ever attempted to influence any member of the House or Senate.

NUC in effect is a shell organization, but for what purpose? Is it possible my stepdad's insurance company is a crooked cog in all of this...whatever it may be? And didn't Benjamin say that his Uncle is the President of another of NUC's member insurance companies? And of course, so would D.I.C.; The Dibble Indemnity Corporation! What could all this possibly have to do with missing limb cases and with a wholesale grommet company? Gotta get a hold of Benjamin now!

Chapter Nineteen

<u>Learning the Ropes</u>
Baby steps first, then walk and then run.
Dr. A.E. Sussman

Ben's Apartment - 1:23 PM (same day)
"Why don't you take your…go wash up and change out of that suit into some more comfortable clothes, dear?" Lucy suggested. "Take the laundry basket with you. That suit needs a good cleaning and pressing. We'll need to get you a laundry hamper…can't believe you don't have one."

"Sure but…"

"No buts, Benjamin. I can't allow you to walk around in public like that, now can I? You desperately need a woman's touch to touch you up so you can…so others will treat you the way you deserve to be treated. And from what I detect from your subtle hints about your present job I would think you need to seriously think about leaving your present employer and finding something you really care about…a career, not a job. Perhaps, we'll have to work on tweaking a few things."

"Tweaking? What needs twee…tweaking Lucy?"

"Well, your constant state of anxiety for one thing and your wardrobe. Don't get me wrong. You're a sweet and quite good looking man. But you come off as a…as a…a…"

"A jerk? That's what everyone called me growing up, including my parents."

"Not what I was going to say. I was going to say, *as a target for those who see kindness and sweetness as a weakness; the bullies and the mean crass heartless of this world."*

"That's very nice of you to tell me, and…and very unsettling as well. You just described *a schnook*! Do you think I'm a schnook?"

"I would imagine that being a schnook's better than being a crook. But, Benny, you're no schnook! I wouldn't want to be around a schnook, crook, jerk, jackass, ninny, nincompoop, fool or a dope. But I want very much to be with you…take care of you and help you overcome all that's standing in your way of living a reasonably happy existence….if you'd allow me to."

"Lucy, you're the best thing that's…the only person who's come into my life who I know can make me smile," Ben admitted. "I'm afraid you'll walk out of my life like so many other people I have…I had feelings for."

Lucy stared at Ben for several silent seconds while childhood memories of mending injured birds' wings, feeding stray cats and adopting homeless dogs flashed in her mind. Ben, unlike the earlier men in her life, was warm, caring and adorable. She wanted so much to remove his fearful anxieties, shore up his latent inner strength and boost his self confidence. Lucy hugged Ben tightly as if to prevent him from crumbling into a thousand pieces. "I'll never leave you, you silly goose!" she wept.

"Does that mean…do you think a beautiful and smart woman like you could ever fa…fall in love with a loser like, um…like me Lucy?"

Pulling back and holding onto his arms she smiled and said, "We'll talk about all of that later my new friend. You don't know me, *really know me*, now do you? Besides, you might find real happiness with a younger…a girl closer to your age.

I'm old enough to be your...your older sister."

"But what does that have to do with...?" Ben pouted.

"Just saying that you should get over your fears and start going out with a variety of women before you settle for a thirty-two year old divorcée. That doesn't mean I won't...You know what? Why don't you be a good boy and wash up while I prepare us some lunch with what you brought from my apartment. Then I can change out of this stupid waitress uniform while you go to the Titanic Supermarket around the corner so we can fill up that new fridge. I'll give you a list. Think about what you'd like me to make you for dinner while you're in the shower."

"Okay, Luce."

*

Earlier the same day @ 9:36 AM
The National Underwriters Consortium
Corvina Wuff was stunned by what just happed. Was it a double cross or merely a change in plans that Brewster Piffle, her new *benefactor*, made without consulting her?

She thought as she rode down the elevator to the underground parking garage;
Might be for something better. I was given no reason why they fired me...gave me the boot even after I explained I had been promised a new job...promotion as the new Assistant Personnel Director. On the other hand, why did they hand me such a large severance check? All that dough to a secretary...over a year's salary. Guess my job now is to wait for Brewster to show up at the apartment. He said he would bring the lease...sign it over to me the next time he needs...requires my services. Bet he no longer wants me to work 'cause he's going to bring an en-

A second blow was struck when Corvina asked the garage attendant to bring her her car; a spanking new 1955 Ford Thunderbird convertible Farfel B. Fenton had purchased for her last December.

"Sorry, Ma'am. But that car was…two men came in a tow truck…with papers,'" the parking valet explained. "Your automobile was…was repossessed some…'bout twenty or thirty minutes ago. Tried calling upstairs to warn you but…"

"That's okay Reggie. I didn't actually own it myself," Covina confessed. "Thank you."

A cab driver was leaning against his taxi which was parked curbside Just outside the garage exit. Miss Wuff trudged her full-figured body up the ramp. The cab driver tipped his cap and asked the very pleasingly plump beauty, "Can I take you anywhere Miss? You look like you could use a lift."

"You have no idea mister. Take me home please…Caspar Arms Apartments."

"Sure thing Miss. Name's Mike."

Mike's passenger never made it back to her apartment. In fact, Corvina Wuff was never to be seen again.

Chapter Twenty

<u>Green Eyed Monster</u>

*A good woman inspires a man, a brilliant woman
interests him, a beautiful woman fascinates
him, but a sympathetic woman gets him.*
Helen Rowland

Ben's Apartment (same day) @ 3:35 PM

Lucy busied herself cleaning up the lunch dishes and rearranging the kitchen cabinets and drawers while Ben was out food shopping. All the while she considered what it might be like to have a more intensive and intimate relationship with that slightly younger man.

I'd certainly have a better opportunity of steering his life in a better direction and assisting him in finding a professional therapist or some support group to help him overcome his neuroses. After all, it was what kept me from blaming and berating myself for the way my ex-husband treated me. And Benji is such a cute and sweet guy; Not the kind that comes along very much into an older woman's life.

Lucy was reluctant at first to answer Ben's phone when it began ringing. She figured if it's an important call, the caller would call back later after he's returned. Realizing it might be Ben calling her to ask a shopping related question or to tell her he had been in a grocery store accident, she changed her mind. Picturing a falling shelf and flying canned foods toppling on him gave her the impetus to rush to the phone on the seventh ring.

A woman's voice on the other end, said, "Hello, Ben? Can I come over. There's something important you ought to know."

"Er, oh-uh, I'm terribly sorry. Mr. Howard won't be back for some time," Lucy curtly replied. She thought, *Bet it's that Ingrid. Ben was right. Mrs. Furf is a busybody,* "May I take a message?" she icily continued.

"Who the hell are you?" Selma snapped. "He never told me about living with a woman?"

"Oh, you're his work partner, *Selma Stacks!* Well dearie, no need to get your panties in a twist. I'm a friend who's trying right now to help him piece his wretched life together. From what I know about you...you haven't exactly been very kind to my friend. Now what is it you want?"

"What I want is to come right over there and punch you in your nasty face!"

Before slamming the receiver down, Lucy shrieked, "Great! I wrote that message down for Benjamin...exactly what you just said...the way you said it! I suggest you get out of his life one way or the other!"

A slew of conflicting emotions washed in and out of Lucy's being like the tide on a full moonlit night. Lucy was both angry at herself for reacting so violently and angry at Selma for making such a blatant attempt to manipulate poor sweet Benjamin Howard for yet another time. All at once she began to experience a sunny inner glow; feeling warm and milky inside as thoughts of living the rest of her life with Ben crept across slideshow-style in her imagination.

What should I really tell him when he returns? That I overreacted just because his coworker called to discuss something that was probably work related? Some bit of information most likely about the grommets? Grommets, cringles and eyelets! Of course! The topic we never finished discussing!

3:39 PM

The apartment entryway intercom buzzer buzzed. Lucy pressed the buzzer button to allow Ben inside the building lobby without having to fish for his door key. Lucy waited long enough to hear Ben's voice after it buzzed the third time.

"Hey Lucy! It's me! Ben. Had a little mishap...mishap when I tried to open the front door. Could you please come downstairs and bring the laundry basket? One of the bags split but..."

"Sure. Be right down!" Lucy replied. She grabbed the now empty basket and took to the stairs rather than use the slow moving elevator. She imagined she would find Ben under a pile of smashed jars, spilled juice and milk with all the other produce and meat he just purchased strewn about the entrance hall. But that wasn't the case.

Ben was sitting on one of two lobby benches facing the elevator. He was cradling one torn paper grocery sack in his arms like a soldier carrying a wounded comrade from the battle scene. The other bag was nestled on the bench next to him. There was a big grin on his face when she arrived carrying the laundry basket.

"Bag began splitting apart while I was carrying it into the lobby, Luce. The store was out of folding hand carts so I had no choice but to have the clerk overstuff two bags so I could lug them back here. Guess my luck ran out in time. I'm sure lucky to have you around to..."

"Oh, you poor dear. You really might have called. I could've chanced going around the corner and walking two blocks without being seen by one of Fusty's..."

"Oh, you don't have to worry about Fusty or anyone else from that former fake restaurant," Ben said as they began transferring the groceries into the basket. "The ones who haven't been picked up yet are probably laying low. It was all the talk among the customers, clerks and cashiers at Titanic Foods."

"What was? You spoke to strangers?"

"Uh-huh, First off, you were right. You told me if I walk around with a smile...even if I don't really feel happy, that people will have a different perspective...won't have a negative view about me; avoid me. Yeah! People actually stopped to ask me if I heard what happened to that new coffee shop in the neighborhood. I told them I knew it was shut down this morning for unsanitary conditions. But Lucy, that wasn't the big news. The damn place would have burned down to the ground if it wasn't for a passing policeman catching sight of the owner and another man carrying beer kegs from the alley behind the coffee shop. He stopped them to inspect the kegs on account that they don't have a license to sell alcoholic beverages. It wasn't beer. The kegs were full of kerosene!"

Lucy was speechless. She said nothing until the elevator began its ascent. "That's good to know...that I'm not in any danger but...uh, but Benjamin, there's a little matter I need...I don't want to go home just yet. Can I stay here? There's so much I need to say...tell you. More than just to explain what a cringle is. I need to tell you what...how I feel for you. And I have to ask for your forgiveness for something awful I did while you were shopping."

Ben was unlocking his apartment door when he giggled, "Oh, Lucy! You didn't throw out my favorite tie, did you? I know it has a ketchup stain and all, but I love that tie!"

Lucy took the grocery bag from Ben and placed it on the floor next to the laundry basket. She hugged and passionately kissed him.

"Oh, Benji! I hope you can *love me*...Love Lucy Herzog, with all the stains on her life's permanent record card."

Chapter Twenty-One

<u>Should the Teacher Stand So Near?</u>
All learning has an emotional base
Plato

**3:55 PM (same day)
Telephone booth on corner of
Mt. Vernon Square across the street from:
The Pork Barrel Cafe
1003 7th Street NW, Washington, DC**

The nasty ill-tempered women who hung up the phone had Selma seeing red. She couldn't get it out of her head that, ever though she had no physical attraction to him herself, Ben was having an intimate relationship with another woman. She crossed the street to sit down with a cup of coffee at The Pork Barrel Cafe to plan a new strategy which would not include Benjamin Howard. Still, she couldn't seem to let go of the ob-session of being the one to influence and order Benjamin Howard's comings and goings. Ever since she could remember, Selma deemed it a personal failure to lose even the most worthless of prizes in any game or competition.

Selma nursed two cups of coffee while ruminating:
Imagine! Ben thought I was overbearing! Well I am, when I have to be…when the circumstances call for pushing people aside…usually stupid men, to get what I need to get done. Maybe Benjamin Howard's not who he pretends to be. He may use that down-in-the-mouth gullible sad sack persona to get others to do the hard work…the dirty on the ground, in the mud tasks that make the world go 'round. That's gotta be it! Wonder if that bitch who hung up on me is the same woman he was having dinner with last night? Why would he be more attracted to her than me? Oh, what the hell. Must put my mind on uncovering the real story behind NUC and their associated

Insurance companies. I would love to use the next few days to go back to Jersey and confront my stepdad. But he's already left with Mom for Havana. Wouldn't be surprised if he's writing it off as a business expense and gambling with a good chunk of Inkblatt Indemnity's assets. Wait! Cuba! Maybe he's attending some mobster conference down there...those nightclubs are all owned by the biggest wise guys, Lansky, Luciano and the rest... common knowledge where I grew up. Hmm. We've been dealing with dangerous people all along. Despite Mr. Rhanbyte's orders, I think I'll try snooping around the NUC Building on the weekend. The security guard will let me in as long as I show him my NUC ID. I'm certainly not falling for that ruse about waiting to be called for a personal assignment. If he thinks we're dopes, why would he expect we'd be the best people to do some special work for him? Unless it would be to get us embroiled in something that...some operation for which he and the NUC organization need a couple of fall guys. I ain't stupid enough to follow anything he assigns me to do. Better write down my thoughts and what my plans are, step-by-step. I'll mail it to Benjamin so there'll be a record just in case I don't come out of this alive. The last step in this process will be reporting what I know, have seen and suspect to the FBI. Doubt if they're on the take. Wait! I really should have my phone number changed...or better still, find someplace else to live, because my life won't be worth a plug nickel even if the NUC people can't reach me by phone. They know where I live.

Ben's Apartment (same day) @ 3:51 PM

Ben never felt anything thing like it before. Lucy's kisses were both gentle and volatile. No woman ever made him experience that sensation of pure joy. He felt safe and secure in her arms as his body was ratcheting up for release. But somehow in the heat of passion he knew, as did Lucy, that they needed to slow things down. He may be in love with her but they met less than twenty-four hours ago. Ben wanted a lasting relationship not a one night stand. Jumping into bed with Lucy so early in their relationship, especially because he was so inexperienced might cause the audience of one to walk out before they ring down the curtain.

Lucy was of a different mindset. She was more than certain they were perfect together; that she could coach Ben in how to pleasure a woman just as she had showed him how to properly wipe off a kitchen countertop. Her ex-husband's idea of love making was more of a dry mechanical gym workout, after which she felt like a harpooned beached whale. No tenderness, no laughter, no pillow talk, no expressions of love and no afterglow.

And yet, this time it was Ben who pulled back. "I want to make love to you Lucy...more than anything. But shouldn't we first discuss...are you certain this is the right thing to do...for you? Please don't look like that. I need...we need to consider what's happening. You yourself told me that I don't really know you and...and that I need experience with other women. And I'm convinced that what you said is true. I met you only last night. I don't want to start something that...I'm falling in love with you more and more...each time I look at you. But I'm afraid as you get to know me better you'll discover that I'm not in you league."

"Not in my league? What does that even mean, darling? Sure the age difference thing is there but...but five years, Benji? Women live longer than men. Five years is nothing."

"Yes, exactly. That's just it. When it comes to romance, you're in the Major Leagues and I've barely been in the Minor Leagues. Not even a batboy. Look, I've been sitting on the bench since I reached puberty. You have experience. You've had boyfriends and even a husband. I've had no-one since Nadine Nerfletz, my high school prom date. Outside of some awkward petting...Lucy, I haven't even seen a naked woman in person. How would I expect to meet your expectations in that arena alone?”

“Okay dear man. If you allow me to be with you I...I promise to slow the train of love down to a crawl. Answer this Ben. Did you ever have someone give you lessons after school? Extra help?”

“Yeah. My parents paid a college girl money to help me with algebra. And there was Mr. Livotti who started me out on the clarinet when I was ten. And there was...”

“Great! So think of me as a tutor who will be giving you home schooling of sorts. Heh-heh, you won’t need to find the perfect reed to play your exercises. You may even look forward to doing your homework.”

“Uh-um, I get it. That sounds like a good plan. Don’t spare my feelings if it all doesn’t work out for you, Luce.”

“Our second lesson will be scheduled sometime after dinner. And speaking of dinner, let’s get all that stuff on the floor put away.”

“Don’t you mean our *first* lesson?”

“The first lesson starts right now. There are several parts. I want you to gaze into my eyes when we’re eating dinner tonight. Touch me and kiss me whenever you feel it’s appropriate and I’ll do the same. Later, when we’ve washed, dried and put away all the dishes...you’ll finally have the opportunity of seeing a fully naked woman in person. I hope you’re not disappointed, my special student.”

Chapter Twenty-Two

<u>Peeling the Onion</u>
The more you peel an union the more you cry
Chef Maurice Frontenac

The Pork Barrel Cafe
Same day @ 4:51 PM

Selma was about to pay for the coffee and head back home. But she still needed to find some easy way to break the three year lease she signed less than two weeks earlier. A conversation between two men caught her attention while she was leaving a tip on the table. Two lawyers were discussing a successful legal argument in a renter/landlord dispute. One of the men was describing how he won a case by arguing that his client's father, a New Yorker, was paying the rent for his college student son. The judge dismissed the landlord's law suit on the basis that reciprocity does not exist between New York City Civil Courts and those of The District of Columbia.

Selma walked over to speak to the lawyer. She flashed a flirtatiously disarming smile while leaning over just enough for her décolleté to be at eye level with Herman Snuster, esq.'s gawping face.

"Excuse me sir. I didn't mean to listen in on your conversation. It's just that...you see, my nephew seems to be having...He and my brother are in a similar situation...like the one you just described."

Attorney Snuster slid across his booth seat to make room. He replied, "Why don't you sit right here and tell me what's on your mind, miss?"

Theodore...he's a college student...a Junior at William Blount

University...here in D.C. He's from New Jersey. My brother signed a lease for a studio apartment but it's full of roaches and the noise in the neighborhood at night isn't conducive for studying for his classes. He desperately wants to move to a better place. Do you know if Newark, New Jersey also doesn't have *reprotrocity* with Washington, DC?"

"Ha-ha. Young lady, the word is *reciprocity* and...But you can reassure your brother and nephew that, as far as walking away from the premises without regard to giving a thirty day notice and incurring associated fees, the lease they signed isn't worth the paper it's written on. Of course, his father will have to forgo his security deposit."

"Thank you so much sir. I appreciate that advice!"

Mr. Snuster handed Selma his business card. "Call on me anytime you need legal advice or...or anything else I may do for you," he leeringly smiled.

"Well, maybe there is Mr. Snuster. Are you finished with that newspaper...on the table? I oughta check the real estate section for my dear nephew. Lucky for him his auntie lives nearby."

"Oh, certainly. The afternoon edition of The Post Times Dispatch. Here take it with my best wishes."

"Thanks!"

Thursday, April 7 - Saturday, April 9, 1955

Selma went into manic phase and accomplished quite a lot in very little time. By eleven AM the next morning She already had:

1. Found a smaller but adequate one bedroom apartment in

Columbia Heights; a brownstone far from her present digs

2. Mailed a letter to the rental management company stating that she's leaving the premises. She made sure to note that as a Newark, New Jersey resident her father can legally consider the lease null and void at anytime as long as he forfeits the security deposit

3. Hired a moving company to bring most of her furniture to her new apartment and the remainder to a storage facility

4. Cancelled the utilities

5. Closed her bank accounts and opened new ones at a bank closer to where she was moving

*

1451 Harvard Street NW, Washington, DC

Selma Sachs spent the majority of the next couple of days fixing up and furnishing her new flat. Columbia Heights, unlike where she moved from, felt more like the northern urban environment she was used to. In 1955 it may have been the most diverse neighborhood in what has always been a highly segregated small city. Also, *The Heights* was comprised of mostly blue collar families along with a good smattering of college kids who found the rents more affordable than in the the more tony parts of town.

*

Saturday, April 9th, 8:37 AM
1151 Connecticut Ave. NW

Selma followed through on her plans to visit the National Underwriters Consortium building on the weekend. Other than one or two security personnel and a small maintenance crew, the likelihood of anyone actually working more than a five day work week was minimal at best. She discovered on her arrival that the building was completely shut down.

While pacing back and forth trying to figure out what possibly could have happened, she thought of a detail that should have registered the first day she walked into that office building:

I know it's one of the older nondescript commercial buildings, but...but it hadn't dawned on me that it was quite unusual for a trade organization not to have their name on the outside. Whether it's a small store front or a tall skyscraper, don't most of these groups trumpet to anyone passing by who they are...a sign or logo on the facade of whatever structure they inhabit? Talk about fishy and shifty!

Selma looked up in frozen wonderment at what had been the top floor window of Farfel Fenton's and later, Cooper Rhan-byte's, Private office. "Where the hell are they? she said out loud; her voice echoing on the empty street.

"Excuse me miss. May I have a word with you?" a male voice behind her boomed.

Selma swiveled around on her high heels. A very serious man was holding out his credentials.

"I'm Agent Andrew Weingarten...F.B.I. Can we talk?"

Chapter Twenty-Three

<u>Soft Touch</u>

*The cat is the only animal which accepts the
comforts but rejects the bondage of domesticity*
Georges-Louis Leclerc

**Wednesday April 6, 1955, 8:21 PM
Ben's Apartment**
Lucy was removing the last of the dinner dishes off the
kitchen table when Ben asked, "So Luce, how'd I do so far? A,
B, C, or D?"

"Darling, I didn't mean to make our relationship...our behav-
iors...yours, mine, seem like work...schoolwork. You'll know
how you're doing, as you put it, by the way we naturally react
to one another. Haven't you noticed this smile on my face?"
she winked.

"Yes, of course. I'm pretty sure I have one as well. I'm not
trembling or uneasy around you. This may be the longest
stretch of time I can remember when I'm not obsessing about
some future negative event. Everything small or large would
cause me to focus on the worst possible outcome...usually
something I might have created. But now my one fear is that I
will never, can never learn to be, um-uh...*romantic*. Perhaps
I'm too old...an old dog that can't learn new tricks."

"This is what the movies and books have created...an ideal-
ized version of what love and romance are supposed to be like.
Get it in your head that you can't be, could never and will never be like any of those movie stars, even if you looked like
them, sounded like them, danced and spoke beautiful words
like they've been trained to do. That's all fake. They're pre-
tending to be real people. They're acting and speaking dia-

logue that's written down...from scripts...speaking spoon fed words which are not their own. Be yourself is all I want. I can guarantee you that I'm no Lana Turner or...You know what's really romantic to me, Benjamin?"

"Er-uh-um, Kirk Douglas? Tony Curtis? Robert Taylor?"

"No, silly. What's really romantic, what defines the essence of a romantic partnership is two people working together as a team and enjoying the experience."

"Oh, I get it. Are you going to wash the dishes and am I going to dry them or is it the other way around?"

Lucy giggled and winked, "Hmm. Perhaps getting your hands softened up in warm soapy water might enhance your gentle touch. We still haven't discussed grommets and the grommet industry Ben. I'll tell you more about that after we dry the dishes and utensils and put them away. How's that sound, sweetheart?"

"Sounds soapy. Our own soap opera."

"Now there's an idea! A very romantic one. We can discuss grommets while you explore my body and I yours in a nice warm bubble bath."

"A babble buff...bubble bath?"

"Yeah, darling. A bath in the buff. There's some nicely scented bath powder in the cosmetic case I asked you to bring from my place. I can finish up here in a jiffy. You go turn on the tub and get undressed. Meet you in the bathroom in four minutes."

"But Lucy! I've never been naked in front of anyone before...'cept maybe a doctor."

"Okay, then. I'll just have to undress you myself. You have no idea how a conversation about little metal rings can be so sensuous until you hear me wax poetic about small steel industria components."

"Ooow Just the way you said that has already got me very, um, very excited."

*

Saturday, April 9th, 8:46 AM

"No need to be frightened or concerned Miss...Miss Sachs... Selma Sachs," Agent Weingarten stated. "You're not...not in any official trouble. However, unfortunately, I have bad news for you. Been trying to track you several hours now. If it weren't for the letter your mother left half written on the hotel room desk in Room 53-F of the Hotel Karhumba in Havana, we wouldn't know your name. And Curtis Inkblatt, your stepdad, had a piece of paper in his wallet with a phone number that we traced to this building. He wrote *Selma's office phone* under it. So I came here...walking right behind you. Your face matches the photos your mother had in her wallet. See this

100

one? I picked out the newest one.”

“Oh no! Are they...are my parents okay? Why did you...were you investigating my parents?”

“Anyone who was murdered...the boating party guests were all poisoned. We believe the boating party was staged...they were poisoned and their bodies were arranged on the yacht and there was no sign of a crew, galley staff, or musicians aboard *The Spinnaker.* That yacht must have been carried across the Florida Straits from Havana Harbor to Miami by the Gulf Stream yesterday. Our men, along with the Coast Guard, discovered explosives in the hull and engine compartment. Looks like the timing device never went off as planned. In short, the incident had all the appearance of a mob rubout. Twenty men and their wives and girlfriends gone. Curiously, the men were in the same business. Businesses that local state and federal law enforcement agencies are investigating as I speak.”

“Insurance? Owners of small insurance companies?” Selma Sachs gasped.

“Look. This is no place to discuss this matter. You can help us bring the murderers to justice by cooperating. Here’s my card. Other agents are trying to find anyone else who worked in this building...Whatever it was, it wasn’t a legit operation. Im sure you just got yourself innocently caught up in the tidal wave of crime.”

“Yeah, I’m all wet. That’s for sure.”

“Look kid, be in my office 3:00 PM this afternoon. And, if you know anyone else who worked at 1151 Connecticut Avenue, please bring them with you. It’ll save a lot of leg work on our part and a mound of tax payer dollars.”

"I'll be there, Agent Weingarten.

Shit! How will I pay for rent, food and ...? I'll have to find a real job.

Chapter Twenty-Four

<u>Fragile - Handle with Care</u>

Development is a series of rebirths.
Maria Montessori

Wednesday April 6, 1955, 9:17 PM
Ben's Bathtub

They were embracing when Ben purred into Lucy's ear, "Mmm. To think of all the time I wasted taking a bath with *Quackers* instead a real live woman! A rubber ducky would never do anything close to what you did with my…"

"Oh, you're so funny!" Lucy said splashing him with the sudsy bergamot scented water. "Listen to yourself Benji! The first time I've ever seen you act…"

"Happy!" he inserted. "I'd never joke about anything to do with bodily functions in the past, pleasurable or otherwise. I was brought up to believe the human body was not a thing for enjoyment."

"Who were this people who raised you, Miss Haversham?" Lucy asked.

"Who's Miss Haversham, Luce?"

"Charles Dicken's character from <u>Great Expectations</u>. She wa
Pip's prim and cold guardian who instructed him to steer clear
of emotional attachments...to run away from feelings of love."

"Oh. I'll have to read that book. Let's talk about me another
time. I'm certain it would bore you to death. You promised to
sing the praises of ringlets, eyelets and grommets. Oh, and
cringle's, of course."

Lucy explained while they stepped out of the tub, "You already know what grommets are as well as their tinier cousins,
the eyelet, through which you thread your shoe laces. A cringle
is a large grommet used in sailcloth...to fit a ship's rigging...
through which the ropes are threaded."

"Oh, I see. But you said your family had a..."

"Herzog Tooling & Die, my family's company, manufactured
precision industrial and electronic parts. My grandfather
founded the company in 1899. They had US Government contracts during the First and Second World Wars. That's when
they concentrated on steel grommets and grommet related
items. But then, in 1951 the rug was pulled out from under
Pop's and other established companies. HTD's contracts were
not renewed. It was mainly because of Senator Winslow Tontine's influence that his buddy who owns *World-Wide Grommet Fabricators* was able to receive most of the Federal business during Korean War. WWGF were not then or now manufacturers. They're middlemen who import cheaper products
from overseas...products that have been...that many engineers
suspect caused a great number of deaths...plane crashes...ship
engine malfunctions and electronic equipment failures. So
Herzog Tooling & Die had to close its doors after more than
fifty years in business. Money was tight and Pop couldn't secure a loan large enough to retool the entire operation. Mom
passed away soon after. That's when Pop took his own life. This

was shortly after I left home and married my awful ex-husband. It took years of therapy for me to be able to talk about
this with anyone, Benji. I'm glad I have you to hear my story."

"What have I been complaining about all these years?" Ben
reflected. "Come on sweetie. Let's get to the next part of to-
days curriculum...in the bedroom, I presume. But only if you're
up to it."

"If *your'e* up to it, darling," she corrected. "Hmm. So you are."

*

Thursday, April 7, 1955, 10:43 AM
Hotel Nacioanal
Calle 21 y O, Vedado, Plaza La Habana
Havana, Cuba
Sub-basement Room

One of most well known figures in organized crime rose from
his chair, placed his hands on the conference table and
scanned the faces of the Capo de Capos of the largest crime
families in the United States. His mild mannered businessman
face suddenly morphed into a grim expression as he began addressing his peers.

"The whole insurance operation must be unraveled, leveled and wiped off the face of the earth immediately. As you are well aware, Inky never showed up this week for our Insurance Operation Conference. Our guys in Newark report that Curtis Inkblatt and his wife went missing the other day. We suspect he was confronted by the Feds. It's a good bet they had a plant working in his company; Someone who bugged the the damn place. Uncle Sam is most likely making a deal with Inky Inblatt as I speak. He's going to sing like a bird for some get-out-of-jail card. We gotta first close up NUC and destroy every shred of evidence, every document and make every employee who ain't a family member disappear. Gentlemen, time is of the essence! This work must be done on the local level right now!"

Chapter Twenty-Five

<u>While the City Catnaps</u>

Conflict follows wrongdoing as surely as flies follow the herd.
Doc Holiday

Thursday, April 7, 1955, 1:03 PM
Ben's Apartment

In spite of the NUC non-disclosure agreement he signed Monday morning, Ben spent close to an hour recounting every detail of his working experience as a NUC employee.

"So that's about it Lucy. They expect me back at work Monday morning. I can't help but wonder how they changed personnel so quickly. One head of the department I was working for replaced with another in a flash! And this new guy, Mr. Rhanbyte...who has no information from his predecessor, puts Selma and me on paid leave with the possibility of doing special tasks for him. It's got my head in a spin."

"I think it was a good thing you told me everything about how and why you suspected you were given...loaned out by your uncle's insurance company for a three year assignment to work at the National Underwriters Consortium. And as you know, I've been suspicious about those very same things. I was up much earlier this morning than you but before I even put up a pot of coffee I had a thought. I looked through the D.C. phone book's Yellow Pages. There's no listing for NUC! What do you think that means, darling? As far as I'm concerned there's something more than peculiar about that so called organization...something dangerously criminal, in the least."

"Yeah, but my Uncle Ralph's not crooked!" Ben maintained. "Quibble Surety Company is a real business. I should know, I worked there. They paid for my move to this town, the rent and everything."

"Maybe you were kept in the dark about what was going on at the top. Maybe those three year assignees were actually being sent into exile and not given a prestigious promotional opportunity. You admitted you didn't know what the hell you were doing at Quibble, did you not?"

"Uh-huh. Thought I'd be canned pretty damn soon. I guess I convinced myself that Uncle Ralph saw this as a way to get me trained by the best of them."

"Sweetheart, I've made-up my mind and I hope you'll agree. You must quit now or you may wind up in jail or...or dead! You can move in with me. Don't even make contact with that Selma woman. She may have been in on all of it. We'll find legitimate jobs...anything temporary for now. I still have money in the bank from my divorce and I invested my share of the money Mom left me in her will. We'll get by. Without sounding any more dramatic, you need to move out of here. The people you're dealing with who are running some kind of scam know where to find you."

"I don't know, Luce."

"Get on the phone and call your uncle. Thank him for his help and support but explain you've decided that insurance isn't your field; that you're not returning to New York. Let's see what he says. But stand your ground if you want Lucy Herzog in your life...if you care about us!"

"Okay. I'll call him right now. He's a man of habit. Lunch everyday at 11:45 and back at his desk at one."

Ben went to the phone and dialed his uncle's private number. A recorded message said: *Sorry, this number is no longer in service*. He dialed Quibble Surety's general number and received the same message. He phoned his aunt and uncle's home number In desperation. The line was dead."

"Lucy, you gotta help me get outta here and...and quick!

Chapter Twenty-Six

<u>Casting Fate to the Wind</u>

*The pessimist complains about the wind;
the optimist expects it to change;
the realist adjusts the sails.*
William Arthur Ward

**Saturday, April 9th, 3:13 PM
FBI Headquarters
Department of Justice Building
950 Pennsylvania Avenue NW, Washington, DC**

An imposing figure of a man stepped into the small interrogation room just as Selma Sachs was signing a twelve page double spaced printed transcript of her verbal testimony.

Agent Andrew Weingarten announced, "Director Jervis would like to say a few words to you, Miss Sachs."

"I'm Lance Jervis, Executive Director of our agency's Criminal Investigative Division. Thank you for showing up voluntarily, Miss Sachs and for your testimony regarding everything you witnessed at that fake organization. We handled you a bit differently for two reasons. One, we didn't want to scare you away by some of the details we must disclose to you; and two, you don't seem to have had any direct involvement with the widespread criminal activities that enmeshed you in that den of thieves. We know that you were a typist in one of the member companies, Inkblatt Indemnity, even though your stepfather was the owner and president. I suppose he meant to keep you from getting your hands dirty and to keep a tight rein on you as well. That was something he mentioned to us which we verified from a number of sources."

"He's alive? And my Mother?"

"Oh, yes, yes. They're both fine and well and safe which… which is why I personally wanted to speak to you. But before I get into any of that, why don't we have Agent Weingarten explain what we uncovered about The National Underwriters Consortium and their member insurance companies."

"Yes, please."

"I'll make it as simple as possible. No need to go into all the lurid details," Weingarten began. "It was a clever idea which addressed two concerns organized crime families had. Everyone needs insurance. People have accidents, die and crash automobiles. Why not have a number of seemingly legitimate companies of their own to payout claims with dirty dough. It was a laundering system for millions of dollars which also took care of the loyal soldiers on the ground and their loved ones. But they took it one huge step further. They insured some of their lesser employees…the bums lower on the criminal echelon. They profited from creating accidents…real and fake as a punishment for breaking or ignoring organized crime family codes of conduct. So if you didn't carry out an order you might lose a finger in an industrial accident. If killed, given a false identity…forged ID documents from a deceased or bogus worker. Then they took it to another level by using the same scheme on outsiders. This plot was bound to backfire on them at anytime."

"Oh, I see," Selma said. "And my parents?"

"Your stepdad is a crook alright. Known as Inky Inkblatt among the Mob. He was a lucky enough early bird to be flipped by us first. That's why he's ready to testify in court and that's why there's now one of our least populated states whose population recently increased by two."

"Whadda you mean? You sent them to a Federal prison in some godforsaken...?"

Director Jervis jumped in, "No prison. They're in a form of experimental protective custody called The Witness Relocation Program. We've been given funding to test this new concept for the next eighteen months. Congress may make this a permanent program someday if it proves successful. As such, your parents names have been changed, they have memorized their new biographical backgrounds and were issued a complete set of personal documents. Rest assured that they are safe and secure in an undisclosed location. I suggest that you might accept a similar offer from us and join the program. You'll have a target on your back young lady as soon as the Mob learns your dad is cooperating with us. We might even arrange for you to join your parents, if you prefer."

"Think it over, Miss Sachs," Weingarten added. "However, we'll need your answer within the next forty five minutes if we're to remove any vestige of your life in this town. It must be done very soon."

"I don't need another minute. There's no choice except between a brutal death...a mob rubout or living a quiet life in a dull part of the country...maybe a small city like Butte Montana or Boise Idaho, if I'm lucky. Although it'll grieve me not to have any contact with Mom, I don't think I want to see my stepfather ever again knowing how he destroyed our lives."

Jervis told Weingarten, "Get a team together to clean Miss Sach's place out within the next couple of hours."

"Yessir!" Agent Weingarten quickly replied.

Director Jervis spoke very calmly to the trembling lady, "Sit tight Miss Sachs. This is a new undertaking for us and I know you must be quite overwhelmed by what you learned and what you've been through. We'll try to make this procedure as smooth as possible under these extraordinary circumstances and we'll make every effort to see to your personal needs as we go along."

"Thank you. I've...I've never experienced fear in my life. Every negative event seemed more like a contest...a challenge which I met head on, but this...but this is so...so uncertain. I have no control over what happens. I feel for the first time that my life is a crap shoot played with loaded dice."

"I fully understand. It would be easier for us to deal with you if you had been a criminal. We wouldn't be treating you so gently. So this is what's going to happen. A couple of our associates will be here in a few minutes to process you...photos, fingerprints and all of that. You'll probably be here for two or three days while all the arrangements are being made and we get the okay from a special appointed Federal Judge. Being a weekend, it may take longer than usual. We have a room set aside for you...being set up now. Your meals can be obtained at the cafeteria in the basement level. You'll be issued a special pass. Please be aware that we'll always keep tabs on you under your assumed name. You'll have regular contact with an assigned agent wherever we find the best placement for you... almost as if you're on parole...except that our mission is to keep you safe."

"I see."

"There's just one thing I need to ask you Miss Sachs; something that Agent Weingarten didn't press you on during your sworn testimony."

"What's that sir?" I don't think I left out any details. I have a good memory. Always had."

"We've been at a disadvantage because only a few complete documents were found intact within the so-called NUC building. But we can't imagine from your account that they would have sent you out alone in that investigation of Nutty Nathan's Wholesale Grommet Warehouse and the Dibble Indemnity Company. Surely you had a partner."

"Partner, me? No," Selma lied. She was unaware why.

She asked herself, *Would it help Ben Howard or get him in more trouble if I mentioned his name? That poor sap's living with someone who sounded over the phone as if she was a take charge person. I'm alone. I need the Feds' help. But if anything bad happens to him I'll have to live with that on what passes for my conscience.*

Chapter Twenty-Seven

<u>Abstract Artistic Temperament</u>

*Life is a string tied to a craggy rock. If you yank it too hard
it will snap and the end will be shorter. It is the wise man
who grasps it lightly and follows it to its natural conclusion.*
Quaid Xernaz of Shiraz, <u>The Trail of Wisdom</u>, (948 CE)

Thursday, April 7, 1955, 11:33 PM
Montreal Airport
Romeo-Vachon Blvd N, Dorval, Quebec, Canada

Thurston Lambro, the man formerly known in The United States as Brewster Piffle, easily passed through the short customs line. He had done this many times over the past seven years using his legitimate Canadian Passport.

Thurston headed straight to a wall of pay phones and dialed *Pierre "La Souris" Reynald*, an old colleague who fenced the jewelry Thurston's Toronto teenage gang stole a decade earlier. They had kept in touch over the years.

The phone rang; Pierre's wife Séraphine answered. After an exchange of greetings she called her husband to the phone.

"Thursty! So good to hear you, mon ami!" Pierre responded. "Are you in Toronto or in the States?"

"Nuttin' like that Mousey. I'm at the airport and…and back

here to stay...for good. But things are...have been heating up down there, if you know what I mean. Need a place to lay low for a year or two 'til they cool down some. And a new set of IDs and....and hiding out in Quebec would be the best way to..."

"For you? Of course I will arrange everything. Not good to have some taxi driver see you and know where you're going. I'll send my son Hervé *tout de suite* to pick you up and bring you to my place for a few days."

*

Thursday, April 7, 1955, 1:05 PM
Ben's Apartment
"So here's the thing, Lucy. My rent had been paid by Uncle Ralph...by his company, Quibble Surety. They even paid for the furniture. My name's not on the lease. They rented it as company property with my name added as the tenant. Therefore, I have no legal obligation to remain here. I'll be out on my tush in a few days when the check they sent for the deposit, first month and security bounces...leaving me homeless with no source of income. On top of that, I don't know if the law will be looking for me," Ben excitedly explained.

"Take a deep breath, sweetheart," Lucy cooly advised. "Now's the time to calm down so we can think this thing out clearly. This is what I think we can do. I'm not known to anybody at NUC. That means the trail to you ends right here. Let's gather up the most essential things of yours and we'll bring them to my place. We'll...you'll stay inside a few days while I arrange to empty out my bank account and look for a used car."

"Lucy, a getaway car? I can't let you wipe out your savings."

"You're getting to sound a bit dramatic. I'm not wiping anything out of anywhere. I just have my living expenses in a checking and savings account nearby. Since my divorce I've had to be very careful with my money...very frugal. Most of my money...mostly from investing what I received from Mom's life insurance is in a bank in Wilton, Connecticut. Quite a lot. I was hoping to save it for when I can no longer work or...or for emergencies."

"Wilton? Wilton, Connecticut? Where's that and...and why there?"

"The last piece of family property which was in my mom's name was a summer house in Fairfield County. An early 20th century farm house on 100 acres...on lakefront property. My financial advisor recommended I sell off most of the land and rent out the house to pay for upkeep and taxes."

"So what does this have to do with buying a car? What do you need a car for in this city?"

"Benjamin Howard! That's where we're going to live...get married and live in that house! A perfect place to start our new life together!"

"Wait. Slow down. Married, yes...I'm all for that. But didn't you just say...tell me it was rented out?"

"Was rented. Do you know who Mischa Kabulyansky is?"

"No. A ballet dancer?"

"Kabulyansky is the famous Russian born abstract painter whose paintings go for thousands of dollars. He rented the farm house and barn. He converted the barn to use as a studio and as a school to teach painting to aspiring young talented artists. Unfortunately, he passed away last year from liver disease and heart failure due to his second love, gallons of daily vodka. I went to visit him during his final days in Fairfield County Genral Hospital. I was the only one who did. Being a bit of a curmudgeon nobody else wanted to be around him even when he was at death's door. You know me. I can overlook a sensitive volatile artistic personality for what it really is."

"Other than a bad tempered, rude personality what else could it be?"

"A cry for love and understanding. A demand for attention from a heartless and soulless world that doesn't understand him. It's reflected in every brush stroke, every splotch and smudge he put on canvas."

"Drinking yourself to death and being mad at the world? Couldn't he just as easily and more graciously mailed a greeting card to anyone he had a grievance with?" Ben asked.

"That's what you'd do. For all your cuteness, you don't possess an artistic soul, my friend. Mischa knew he wouldn't last more than a few more days. Two days before he passed away, that broken man sent me a letter in which he told me he's leaving me any of the paintings in the house that had not been sold or designated to be donated to several museums around the world. He sent a copies of that statement to his lawyer and agent. The three works I own were recently released by his estate and are now in the hands of art dealers. They'll be put up for action soon. I expect to make a good amount of money from them."

"Wow! So why did you...why were you working as a waitress? Not that there's anything wrong with..."

"Due to my problems with my husband and then running back and forth to check on old Mr. Kabulyansky, I took off a considerable amount of time from my job with the Department of Labor. Then there were nasty crackpot rumors spread that he was a Communist and was foisting his subversive artistic works in our country to poison the minds of American children. So I decided that I wanted to work for myself...learn the restaurant business from the bottom up. That's why I grabbed that job at Fusty's Coffee Shop."

"Tell me what it is we'll be doing in Connecticut?"

"Do you like ice cream, Benjamin?"

"Who doesn't?"

"There's an ice cream parlor...an old fashion style ice cream parlor for sale in Westport, the upsy-tupsy town just south of Wilton. Not far from Route One...The Boston Post Road. Perfect spot. I've been picking up the Fairfield County Bugle at Union Station every weekend to check on business opportunities near my unrented house. The Lickety Split Ice Cream Parlor's been on the market for three months! I'm sure it needs a lot of renovation. Been there since 1910!"

"Lucy, what do you know about selling ice Cream?"

"Not just selling it...making it! Homemade ice cream! I took a non-credit course in ice cream making at Rutherford B. Hayes

Junior College. You'll get to try some of my creations when we're nestled together in my flat."

"Can't wait! I better start packing my things. Hope we can avoid running into old Mrs. Furf!"

Lucy smiled, "Don't take...er-um, Please leave most of your clothes behind, dear. I'll buy you a completely different wardrobe."

"Can I take my favorite tie?"

"Only if you promise to wear it under your ice cream parlor apron."

Chapter Twenty-Eight

<u>Mr. & Mrs. Lickety Split</u>

It's never too late to be who you might have been.
George Eliot

Saturday, August 16, 1969, 12:43 PM
The Lickety Split Ice Cream Parlor
31 Charles Street, Westport, Connecticut

Russel Anderson left I-95 via exit 17 to look for a place to grab a quick bite before continuing back to his empty house in Scarsdale, New York. He had driven to Wabanaki Lake Summer Camp in Lostinda Woods, Maine the day before to visit his daughter Karen. The exit ramp took him onto Saugatuck Avenue. A few streets ahead he noticed a line around the corner of what looked like a restaurant on Charles Street. As he approached closer it became clear to him that the line was merely for ice cream from the Lickety Split Ice Cream Parlor's take out window. A sign announced *sandwiches, burgers and seating inside*. He turned into the small parking lot and parked his shiny new Lamborghini Miura.

The restaurant part of the business was nearly as popular as the ice cream take out window. So Russ sat down on a counter stool. The burger and fries did not disappoint. Though not a big fan of deserts, Russell very much wanted to try the ice cream. He was always looking for small businesses in which to invest his money and help them grow into successful popular brand companies. Ice cream might fit well into his expansive portfolio in which he owned good size shares of supermarkets and fast food chains.

Russel Anderson asked the waiter to bring him one child-size scoop of each of the 23 flavors. "And don't worry young man, I won't have a heart attack," he assured Gordon Pennington, the bewildered summer job teenager. "I merely want to sample each one."

"Can't do that, sir."

"Why not son? I'll pay for all of it if that's what you..."

"Oh no, Nothing like that. The owners insist that we give out free tasting samples to any customer who want to try the variety of ice cream flavors. Here's you bill. Go over to the ice-cream section after you pay the cashier. I'll tell Betty that you want to taste all the ice cream flavors. she'll hand them to you you on a small wood spoons."

"Thanks kid! Here's five bucks for your excellent service."

"Wow!"

"Say, you mentioned the owners of this place. What are their names and how can I get in touch with them?"

"They'll be back here in a couple of hours, sir."

"Here's my business card. Please tell them to call me on Monday morning. I may have something of great interest for them."

Russ had second thoughts about rushing back to his very large empty house. Even the help was away on summer vacation. Tending to entrepreneurial concerns had taken a backseat to his interests and activities ever since he suddenly became a single parent. The ice cream he just sampled kickstarted his hands-on commercial spirit.

Besides, Karen loves ice cream, he laughed to himself. *Hmm. I wonder what she'd think if I put her face on the label of a top selling desert product?"*

So Mr. Anderson decided to stroll around the streets of Westport for a couple of hours and speak face-to-face with whoever owns that little goldmine with the silly name.

*

Same Day - 1:20 PM
13 Skunk Lane, Wilton, Connecticut

Ben and Lucy spent a good part of the late morning/early afternoon overseeing the new larger size ice cream batch freezers being installed in their home factory which had formerly been an artist studio and a dairy barn half a decade before.

The manufacturer's representative had followed behind the delivery truck so he could instruct the proprietors and their two employees how to operate the top-of-the-line state-of-the-art equipment.

"I hope this will help us keep up with the increasing demand," Lucy said to her husband.

"Say goodbye to hand cranking. After fourteen years, make that *good riddance*. Best of all, Mr. Swenson demonstrated that automatic machine cranking didn't affect your formula or change the taste, quality or consistency of our product."

"Send ya folks a bill next week!" Mr. Swenson said as Ben signed an invoice. "Best be gettin' on my way. Call if you have any questions."

"Let's get back to the shop, Luce," Ben told her. "We're short of help with all those college kids leaving for school this week."

"Yes, dear. You're the boss."

Chapter Twenty-Nine

<u>New Name, New Game</u>

*And the day came when the risk to remain tight in a
bud was more painful than the risk it took to blossom*
Anais Nin

Saturday, June 5, 1971, 9:54 AM
174 North Main Street, Kalispell, Montana

  Mrs. Jane Davis arrived early so she'd able to stand at the
front of the crowd. She had been planning two separate
events. Her husband Rick's restaurant would be catering the
cast party for her production of <u>The Pajama Game</u> at the
Kalispell Regional Theater after July 7th's final performance.
The other celebratory event will be for the kids in her drama
class at East Valley Junior High School. She thought that a large
ice cream cake would make the perfect farewell treat for the
last day of school. She took out the flyer from her handbag
which had been distributed in every copy of <u>The Kalispell Ob-
server</u>.

It was a warm day. She thought back to her past life on the East Coast, *Must be in the high 80's there. I probably would be wearing a tee shirt and shorts by now instead of flannel shirts and dungarees through the middle of July.*

The grand opening was slightly delayed. She observed the workmen having difficulty setting up the microphone while a long wide shiny blue ribbon was being fastened across the new stand-alone shop's entrance door. The crowd behind her indicated that this will be a popular business. *Why not? They've been popping up left and right all over the country*, she mused.

At last, Mayor Corky Reynolds walked up to the the microphone.

"Friends, honored guests and all citizens of Kalispell and neighboring towns and villages," he began. "It gives me great pleasure and pride to have helped to strengthen the economy of our fair city during my administration by attracting new businesses and supporting the small shop owners who make up the commercial backbone of our town. You might say that today's dedication of the first franchise of this popular nation-wide chain of ice cream shops in our beloved state and the hundredth in the Country, will be the cherry on the top of the sundae...heh-heh. To cut the grand opening ribbon will be KC Ice Cream Shop franchise owner Harry Hartley. Standing at Harry's left is Mr. and Mrs. Benjamin Howard and Mr. Russel Anderson the owners of Lucy Enterprises of which KC Ice

Cream is a subsidiary."

Jane gasped in shock while a score of local and state news photographers were flashing their cameras. She screamed under her breath, *Oh my God! That's that loser...Ben and his...and his wife!*

ACKNOWLEDGEMENTS

I wish to express my gratitude to

my crack team of "Typo Hunters",

Paul Humbles

Robert Levine

Robert Mattsson

Jack Moscou

Judy Oster

Bobcatbooks
@bobcatbooks.Net

A special thank you to Trebor Retso
for his wonderful illustrations!

Learn about these other titles at
bobcatbooks.net
and

amazon.com

*

Strictly by the Book
Whispers in the Dark
Puzzle Pieces
Perfidious Rogues
The Mystique
The Contractor
Watch Your Step
The Songbird Sings a Deadly Tune
The Acorn Squash Murders
Dagnabbit!
The Templeton Files
Not for Nothing
Appointment in Utopia
Recipe for Death
Free Range Malice
The Maltese Mystery Meatloaf

www.ingramcontent.com/pod-product-compliance
Lightning Source LLC
Chambersburg PA
CBHW031333160726
47993CB00002B/649